ON THE HILL

ON THE HILL

A PEOPLE'S GUIDE TO CANADA'S PARLIAMENT

HEATHER ROBERTSON

M&S

Canadian Cataloguing in Publication Data

Robertson, Heather, 1942–
   On the hill

ISBN 0-7710-7554-5

1. Canada. Parliament – Handbooks, manuals, etc.
2. Parliament Buildings (Ottawa, Ont.) – Handbooks,
manuals, etc.* 3. Canada - Politics and government –
Handbooks, manuals, etc. I. Title.

JL136.R63 1992   328.71   092-09396-6

Printed and bound in Canada. The paper used in this book is acid-free.

McClelland & Stewart Inc.
The Canadian Publishers
481 University Avenue
Toronto, Ontario
M5G 2E9

PAUL VON BAICH

Preface

Canadians take parliamentary democracy for granted, but while we argue ceaselessly and vigorously about political issues, many Canadians have only the vaguest idea of how Parliament actually works. Within the last thirty years, passionate debates over a new Canadian flag, constitutional amendments, a Goods and Services Tax, free trade with the United States, and the unique character of the province of Quebec, have put Parliament under unprecedented public scrutiny, yet the process of government is visible primarily on television. On the news we see the prime minister being mobbed in the hall by shouting reporters, and during Question Period we watch members of Parliament hurl verbal abuse at their opponents across the floor. As a result, many people have come to view Parliament as a crude wrestling match that has little relevance to their own lives and problems.

In reality, nine-tenths of the business of Canada's Parliament takes place away from the public eye, where politicians and their staff work very hard. One million tourists visit Parliament Hill every year, but tours are restricted to a specific area of the Centre Block, the Peace Tower, and four historic offices in the East Block. Apart from the public galleries in the chambers of the House of Commons and the Senate, the rest of the Parliamentary precinct is closed. Visitors must have an appointment; many areas of the Commons and Senate are never seen except by the people who work there.

Parliament Hill has many of the characteristics of a medieval walled city, with a complex and mysterious set of traditions, rituals, and patterns of speech that reflect its origins deep in British history. While many of these arcane practices are essential to the functioning of a parliamentary democracy, they are often incomprehensible to a twentieth-century observer.

An alphabetical guide to Canada's Parliament, *On The Hill* provides brief, basic information about the rules and rituals and history of the House of Commons and the Senate, details about the stone carving, stained glass, and gargoyles that make Canada's Parliament Buildings among the finest examples of Gothic Revival architecture in the world, and a peek behind-the-scenes into the daily lives of the four thousand men and women, from cleaners to cabinet ministers, who work on the Hill.

The entries are cross-referenced, with the relevant other topics printed in capital letters, so that one entry leads automatically to the others. Since the overwhelming majority of MPs, senators, and governors general are men, they are referred to as "he," however an entry on "Women" describes their increasing influence in federal politics.

On The Hill is a general reference, not an encyclopedia or textbook – literature dealing with procedure alone would fill a library – and readers looking for more information may wish to consult the following: *Annotated Standing Orders of the House of Commons,* Queen's Printer; *How Canadians Govern Themselves,* by Eugene Forsey, Government of Canada; *The Parliament of Canada,* by C. E. S. Franks, University of Toronto Press; *Rideau Hall: An Illustrated History of Government House,* by R. H. Hubbard, McGill-Queen's University Press; *Speakers of the House of Commons,* by Gary Levy, Library of Parliament. Books of photographs include: *Canada's Parliament,* by W. J. L. Gibbons and others, text by Philip Laundry, House of Commons; *Residences: Homes of Canada's Leaders,* by Maureen McTeer, Prentice-Hall Canada; *Statues of Parliament Hill,* by Terry Guernsey, National Capital Commission; and *Stones of History: Canada's House of Parliament, A Photographic Essay,* by Chris Lund and Malak, National Film Board. An article on the East Block, "The Pride of Parliament," by R. J. Phillips, appeared in *The Review,* Imperial Oil Ltd., #4, 1983. Both the Senate and Public Information Offices produce free brochures and fact sheets, and the governor general's office supplies an information kit.

I am grateful for the enthusiasm and co-operation of the Speaker of the House of Commons, John Fraser, and for the assistance of the House of Commons staff and the Senate Information Office. I am also grateful to Perrin Beatty, the Minister of Communications, and Liberal MP John Harvard for permission to photograph their offices. My particular thanks to Duncan Cameron, professor of political science at the University of Ottawa, and Professor William Neville of the University of Manitoba for reviewing the manuscript.

Heather Robertson
Toronto, 1992

A

Act

Once a bill is passed by both the House of Commons and the Senate and has received royal assent from the governor general it becomes an act of Parliament and the law of the land. The new law goes into force immediately unless a specific future date is set. One copy of the act is printed on heavy vellum paper and stored in the Clerk's vault; mass-produced copies may be obtained from the QUEEN'S PRINTER. *See also:* BILL, SENATE, ROYAL ASSENT.

Aides

Members of Parliament have at least one aide or executive assistant to help them organize their offices, write speeches, and respond to their constituents' requests. Aides are hired by the MPs and their principal qualification is fierce party loyalty. Aides do all the work MPs don't want to do or have no time for, and a member's reputation often rests on his aides' abilities. Ambitious aides may become MPs themselves, or marry MPs (*see:* SCANDAL). Aides are usually young, energetic, competitive, and gregarious (*see:* GOSSIP, PRESS GALLERY). Male aides tend to favour striped shirts and suspenders, females short hair and flat shoes; both are easy to spot by their bright eyes, big smiles, and air of importance.

Architecture

The architectural style of the Parliament Buildings is usually described as Gothic Revival or Victorian Gothic, a style very popular in England when the plans for Canada's new houses of Parliament were drafted in 1859, although all the architects, Thomas Fuller and Chilion Jones (Centre Block) and Augustus Laver and Thomas Stent (East and West blocks), were residents of Canada. Designed by two different firms, the three original buildings were very similar in scale and ornamentation; the variegated Nepean sandstone of the outer walls was set off by grey slate roofs and the wood trim was painted Chinese blue. After

Canada's Parliament Buildings are among the finest examples of Gothic Revival architecture in the world.

T. ATKINSON / NCC / CNN

the Centre Block was destroyed by fire in 1916, it was replaced by a more austere and imposing building designed by John Pearson of Toronto and J. O. Marchand of Montreal. With its 300-foot Peace Tower dominating Parliament Hill, the present Centre Block is three storeys higher than the original and lacks the red sandstone detailing around the windows, a choice Pearson made against such voluable protests from members of Parliament the final decision was left to the governor general.

Canada's Parliament Buildings are not replicas of the British Parliament at Westminster but are original and eclectic designs derived from the medieval architecture of England and Europe. The towers are Germanic in origin, the mansard roofs French, the pointed windows Italian, and the library is modelled on an English chapter house. The Gothic Revival style is characterized by soaring towers, flying buttresses, vaulted roofs, pointed arches, roughhewn stone, and a delight in ornamentation that reflects the craftsmanship of the artisans. Gothic is a creative and individual style. On Parliament Hill no two towers are the same design or dimensions, windows are round, arched, or rectangular, doorways differ in height and width, and the uneven façade is broken by buttresses, dormers, porticos, and niches. The original slate roofs have been replaced by copper that turns green with age. Inside, the finishing combines a dozen different kinds of stone and marble, oak, pine, teak, walnut, and ebony woods, plaster, wrought iron, hand-painted linen, murals, paintings, and stained glass, as well as modern carpet, wallpaper, and vinyl.

Twenty-three designs for the buildings were originally submitted, sixteen for the Centre Block, seven for the East and West blocks. They varied from Gothic to Classic, Italian, Norman, and Plain Modern. The Classic designs would have made Ottawa look more like Washington, D.C., than London, England, but they were rejected as too expensive. Not only did the Gothic style reflect the origins of Parliament in the Middle Ages but it was ideally suited to local materials and the rugged, natural site. An organic style, with shapes and motifs derived from nature, Gothic captured the spirit of the Canadian wilderness and the aspirations of a young nation. So many distinctively Canadian

The original, smaller Centre Block was built in the 1860s and destroyed by a spectacular fire in 1916.

symbols, figures, and emblems have been incorporated into the buildings their architecture is perhaps most accurately called Canadian Gothic. Canada's Parliament buildings are considered the most interesting and vital example of Gothic Revival architecure in North America. *See also*: BUILDINGS, CENTRE BLOCK, EAST BLOCK, GARGOYLES, HILL, HISTORY, INTERIOR DESIGN, LIBRARY, MEMORIAL CHAMBER, PEACE TOWER, RENOVATION, ROTUNDA, STAINED GLASS, STATUES, STONE CARVINGS, WEST BLOCK, WOOD CARVINGS, WROUGHT IRON.

Canada's coat of arms.

Arms of Canada

Canada's coat of arms is flanked by the lion and the unicorn, ancient heraldic symbols of England and Scotland, and by two flags, the Union Jack and the Fleur-de-lis, emblems of the two nations that originally claimed sovereignty over the "New World" of North America: France in 1535, England in 1763. The emblems on the shield are, clockwise: the three lions of England, the lion rampant of Scotland, the fleur-de-lis of France, and the harp of Ireland; the three maple leaves at the bottom symbolize Canada. The Crown above the shield means that Canada is a constitutional monarchy. The Latin inscription, which translates as "From Sea Unto Sea," reflects the fact that Canada borders on three oceans, the Atlantic to the east, the Pacific to the west, and the Arctic to the north. The Arms of Canada do not represent Canada's original inhabitants, the native Indians and Inuit, nor the hundreds of thousands of Canadians who have more recently come from central and eastern Europe, Italy, Greece, Portugal, Russia, India, Pakistan, Africa, the Middle East, China, Southeast Asia, South and Central America, the West Indies, and the United States.

Thomas D'Arcy McGee.

NATIONAL ARCHIVES OF CANADA / C-51976

Assassination

Late on the night of April 7, 1868, Thomas D'Arcy McGee, an Irish-born member of Parliament and a cabinet minister, was shot dead outside his boarding house on Sparks Street in Ottawa. The assassin fled. There were no witnesses, but the murder was believed to be the work of Irish Fenians, who resented McGee's support for British rule. An Irish immigrant, Patrick James Whelan, was tried for McGee's murder, convicted, and hanged on February 11, 1869, although Whelan protested his innocence until the end. McGee is the only Canadian member of Parliament to have been assassinated. Canada abolished capital punishment in 1976.

B

Backbencher

A member of Parliament's status is measured by his place in the HOUSE OF COMMONS. The prime minister and his cabinet ministers sit in the centre of the front rows to the Speaker's right, the leaders of the opposition parties and their "shadow" cabinets in the front rows to the Speaker's left. Parliamentary secretaries, caucus officers, and up-and-coming MPs who have caught their leader's eye occupy the middle rows, all the rest are backbenchers or private members. Freshman MPs usually sit in the top rows of the back benches, the Independents and minority parties farthest from the Speaker, and most move down towards the front as they are re-elected. Some MPs remain backbenchers for years, unknown to the country at large but popular with their constituents. *See also*: MEMBERS OF PARLIAMENT, PARTIES, WHIP.

Bar

I nside the main doors to the Commons and Senate chambers a brass railing bars visitors from proceeding farther without permission from the SERGEANT-AT-ARMS or BLACK ROD. The Bar symbolizes the privacy and PRIVILEGE of both houses: senators are not allowed to enter the Commons chamber, members of Parliament may not enter the Senate. Senators, MPs, or private citizens may be summoned to appear at the Bar to explain words or actions Parliament considers to be contemptuous of its honour and integrity, however this power is rarely used: complaints are usually referred to a committee, where they are quietly resolved. As the highest court in the land, Parliament may arrest and imprison anyone it finds in contempt. In 1913 Mr. R. C. Miller refused to answer questions

The Speaker of the House of Commons, accompanied by the Clerk and the Sergeant-at-Arms bearing the mace, stands at the Bar of the Senate during the Opening of a session of Parliament.

CANAPRESS

before the public accounts committee and the House of Commons; he was committed to the Carleton County Jail until the end of the session. To prevent thin-skinned politicians from crying "Off with his head!" over every slight, the Speaker of the Commons has remarked that "something can be inflammatory, can be disagreeable, can even be offensive, but it may not be a question of privilege unless the comment actually impinges on the ability of members of Parliament to do their job properly." In practice, MPs and senators are subject to severe criticism, ridicule, malice, and abuse, and most accept it as an unavoidable part of public life.

Barber

Among the many PERKS enjoyed by MPs are the services of two barbers and a hairdresser on Parliament Hill. The barbershop is often criticized as a frivolity, but it is a very spartan, old-fashioned facility located in the basement of the Centre Block. The barbers and hairdresser are employees of the House of Commons and their modest fees go into the public treasury.

Beaver

The beaver is Canada's official national emblem. An ugly, energetic, bark-eating rodent famous for its big teeth and flat tail, the beaver owes its prestige to Canada's origins in the fur trade with Europe. The trapping and trading of furs was Canada's first inland economy, and in the eighteenth and nineteenth centuries the beaver's dense, soft fur was prized for the making of felt hats. In early Canada a beaver skin was a recognized currency, and today the beaver appears on the Canadian five-cent coin. Legend has it that Canada's Great Beaver lives on Parliament Hill, guarded by the Keeper of the Beaver, but the Great Beaver has never been seen.

Bill

Draft legislation presented to Parliament for debate and approval is called a bill. A bill is introduced to the House of Commons by a cabinet minister or private member and given *first reading* without debate. It is then read a second time, followed by days or weeks of debate and a vote on its principle. If the bill passes *second reading*, it is examined in detail by an all-party committee of MPs whose duty is to criticize it, propose amendments, and report back to the House. After the bill has been discussed and amended at this *report* stage, it is read a *third* time, followed by a shorter debate and a vote. If the bill is passed, it goes to the Senate for further study and debate; the Senate may also introduce bills that go on to the House of Commons. The Senate may delay a bill or send it back to the Commons for revision. If the Commons refuses to accept the Senate's recommendations, the bill can be withdrawn or returned to the Senate a second time: if the Senate still refuses to pass it, the bill dies. Once a bill is passed by both Houses of Parliament it becomes law as soon as it receives royal assent. A bill can take months or years to make its way through the stages of debate and approval; only 70 per cent of the government bills introduced to

Parliament are passed. Until House rules were changed in 1986 almost no private members' bills became law; today twenty are selected for debate and votes are held on six. *See also*: ACT, COMMITTEES, DEBATE, GOVERNMENT, PROCEDURE, ROYAL ASSENT, SENATE, VOTE.

Bill of Rights

When Canada became a self-governing dominion within the British Empire in 1867, Canadians assumed they would enjoy the rights and freedoms guaranteed by British law and custom. This was not always the case in practice, and in 1960 the Canadian House of Commons clarified those "human rights and fundamental freedoms" in a Bill of Rights, guaranteeing all Canadians, without discrimination with regard to race, national origin, colour, religion, or sex: (a) the right of the individual to life, liberty, security of the person and enjoyment of property, and the right not be be deprived thereof except by due process of law (b) the right of the individual to equality before the law and the protection of the law (c) freedom of religion (d) freedom of speech (e) freedom of assembly and association (f) freedom of the press. *See also*: CHARTER OF RIGHTS AND FREEDOMS.

Black Rod

CANAPRESS

Black Rod

The Gentleman Usher of the Black Rod performs a ceremonial role in the Senate similar to that of the SERGEANT-AT-ARMS in the House of Commons. Originally the king's deputy, he carries a stout ebony rod as the symbol of his authority, and he uses the rod to rap on the door of the Commons chamber to summon MPs to the Senate for the OPENING of Parliament or royal assent. Black Rod is also responsible for the security of the Senate.

Board of Internal Economy

Home to 295 MPs and a total staff of approximately three thousand, the House of Commons is a large corporation with an annual budget over $230 million. The head of the household is the Speaker, "Mother" as he is sometimes jokingly called, and when he is not trying to preserve order among unruly MPs, he is worrying about the grocery bills and the cost of soap. The Speaker chairs the Board of Internal Economy, a committee of nine MPs, which is responsible for the efficient daily management of the House. The board approves all expenses, although the work is carried out under the authority of the Administrator, the CLERK, and the SERGEANT-AT-ARMS. *See also*: BUDGET, STAFF.

Bomb

On May 16, 1966, Paul Chartier, a forty-five-year-old trucker from Alberta, walked into the Centre Block as a human bomb. Chartier, who blamed the country's problems on politicians, had enough dynamite strapped to his body to blow up most of the front-benchers in the Commons chamber. Chartier hid in the washroom next to the prime minister's office and lit the fuse, but the fuse was too short. Chartier blew himself up before he could leave the washroom. He is immortalized as the Mad Bomber of Parliament Hill. *See also*: LAVATORIES, SECURITY.

Books of Remembrance

The names of 114,710 Canadians killed in combat outside Canada since Confederation in 1867 are inscribed alphabetically in five Books of Remembrance in the MEMORIAL CHAMBER. The names are handwritten, giving rank and regiment, and the pages are beautifully illuminated. Every morning at 11:00 a.m. a page of each book is turned so that every name is displayed at least

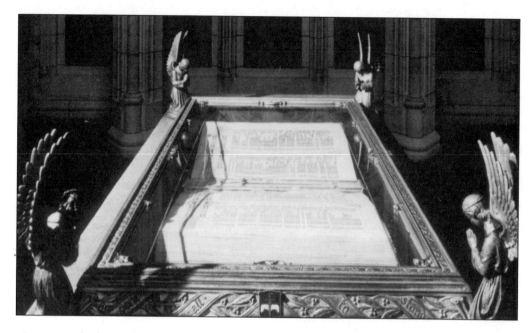

An open Book of Remembrance lies under glass on the main altar of the Memorial chamber. A page is turned every day.

CHRIS LUND / NATIONAL ARCHIVES OF CANADA / PA-185329

once a year. The most recent war commemorated in a Book of Remembrance is the Korean War (1950-53). Canada did not go to war against North Vietnam in the 1960s and suffered no casualties in the war against Iraq in 1991. Canada suffered the highest losses in the First World War (1914-18), in which 66,655 men and women were killed, and this Book of Remembrance rests on the main altar of the Memorial chamber. The chamber also contains a tribute to Canadians who have served in the United Nations peacekeeping forces.

British North America Act

In 1867 the British Parliament passed an act, drafted by Canadians, making Canada the first self-governing nation in the British Empire. The new Dominion of Canada was not entirely independent: the British government technically retained veto power over Canadian legislation and expected Canada to defer to Britain in matters of defence and foreign policy. Political controversies created by this ambiguous relationship with the "mother" country led to complaints from Canadian prime ministers, and in 1931 the British government passed the Statute of Westminster giving Canada fully independent and equal status as a member of the British Commonwealth of nations owing a common allegiance to the CROWN. *See also*: CONFEDERATION, CONSTITUTION.

Budget

The House of Commons has an annual budget of more than $230 million; the Senate $43.4 million. More than half of this money is spent on salaries and expenses for MPs and senators. The other major expense is the cost of doing business: clerks, printing, paper, reporting, messengers, and committee services. Both the House of Commons and the Senate have developed from part-time gentlemen's pursuits into large, self-governing corporations. *See also*: BOARD OF INTERNAL ECONOMY, SENATE.

Buildings

Construction of the Parliament Buildings was undertaken with astonishing and reckless haste, given the size, importance, and complexity of the project. On May 7, 1859, the Department of Public Works invited architects to submit their detailed plans for buildings to house the government of the United Provinces of Canada by August 1. Twenty-three designs were submitted; the winners (*see*: ARCHITECTURE) were chosen by September, the contractors hired in November, and construction began in April 1860. Only then was it discovered that among many other omissions the plans neglected to provide for heat and ventilation, so another contractor was hired to design a central heating system. All three buildings were to be finished by July 1862 at a total cost of $540,000.

When the foundations were dug, the limestone of the Hill was found to be full of fissures and had to be reinforced, and as work proceeded, the Public Works Department demanded countless changes in the architects' plans. By September 1861 the entire budget had been spent and the outer walls were only

The original Centre Block under construction in September 1863. The sheds on the site included a first-aid station for injured workers.

NATIONAL ARCHIVES OF CANADA / C-000773

a few feet high. The delay and expense caused an uproar among the politicians, who refused to pay the architects' and contractors' fees, and construction was suspended for nearly a year; work on the Library did not begin again until 1870. In 1863 a royal commission appointed to investigate the project revealed serious mistakes, misunderstandings, and waste, yet it was too late to stop work and construction went ahead. Cabinet ministers and their staff were able to move into the East Block and West Block in the fall of 1865, and the first session in the new buildings opened on June 8, 1866. By July 1, 1867, Confederation day, the total cost had reached $2,723,981.68. The Library, still the most beautiful of all the buildings, was finished in 1876 at a cost of $300,000.

Although the Parliament buildings were criticized at the time for being too large and extravagant, they almost instantly became crowded and obsolete. The heating system – hot- and cold-air ducts cut through the stone walls – kept the offices at a frigid ten degrees Celsius in the winter, and cabinet ministers and their secretaries huddled by their fireplaces. Public Works specified the "internal furnishing to be plain and substantial, cornices to be put only in the principal rooms and halls." The status of a minister could be measured by the amount of decoration in his office, and except for the Privy Council room and the prime minister's office, it was very little. The interior walls of the original buildings were plaster or wood panelling, the wood floors were covered with carpet or cocoa matting, and the furniture was functional. The fourteen-foot ceilings made the rooms dark at night in the era of gas lighting, but during the day there was plenty of natural light. The CENTRE BLOCK had three interior courtyards; both the EAST BLOCK and WEST BLOCK were built in an L-shape, so every office had an exterior view. Windows were large and numerous – even hallways had windows at each end – and the various shapes and glazing of the windows added character to the lighting of the buildings.

A west wing and the Mackenzie Tower were added to the West Block in 1874, another wing to the north enclosed a central courtyard in 1905, and in 1910 a wing was added on the northeast side of the East Block. The Mackenzie Tower fell down shortly after it was built, confirming suspicions that the contractors had cheated on their work, and after the Centre Block burned down in 1916 (*see*: FIRE) it was found that the standing walls were too weak and shoddy to be built upon (*see*: PATRONAGE). The new Centre Block, built between 1916 and 1920, is three storeys higher than the original and contains much more floor space – 328,000 square feet compared to 223,000 square feet. Including the PEACE TOWER, which was finished in 1927, it cost $12,379,846. Reconstruction and renovations to all three original buildings have amounted to nearly twenty times the original cost, a hundred times the original estimate. Most of the money was spent on hiring thousands of stone cutters and labourers, although in the nineteenth century labourers worked for less than a dollar an hour. The stones were cut by steam power in a huge shed to the east of Parliament Hill, hauled to the site by horse-drawn wagons, and hoisted into place by pulleys. So many men were injured on the job that a small infirmary was set up near the Centre Block. A two-storey workshop was built on the west side of the Hill at the corner of Bank and Wellington streets; when construction was complete it became the home of the Supreme Court of Canada and later the first National Gallery; the workshop was torn down in the 1950s for a parking lot. *See also*: ARCHITECTURE, STONE CARVING.

Bureaucracy

A usually derogatory and contemptuous word for the CIVIL SERVICE, it is customarily described as a *bloated* or *entrenched bureaucracy* peopled by *faceless bureaucrats* and led by *mandarins*, although words like lazy, stupid, idiotic, and more profane descriptions are popular with the public. Because government is Ottawa's biggest industry, it has a large population of bureaucrats.

Bus

Since many MPs and parliamentary staff have their offices across from the Hill on Wellington and Sparks streets, a fleet of small green or silver buses travels a perpetual circle from the Centre Block to the West Block, the Wellington building,

The parliamentary buses are a popular mode of transportation on the Hill, especially in winter.

MONE CHENG PHOTOGRAPHY STUDIO

and the East Block. Riding the bus saves time walking, particularly in the winter when the temperature in Ottawa is often minus fifteen Celsius and the streets are deep in slush. The green buses are for House of Commons personnel; the silver for senators. *See also*: GREEN.

C

Cabinet

The political party that wins the support of the majority of the 295 members of the House of Commons forms the government, and more than thirty government MPs representing all areas of the country are chosen by the prime minister to be members of his cabinet. The word derives literally from cabinet or closet, a small room in the royal palace where the king met in secret consultation with his closest advisers. The king's place is now taken by the prime minister, who relies on a cabinet of elected advisers, but the deliberations of the cabinet remain secret. The cabinet determines government policy, and cabinet ministers are expected to be united in their support for that policy. A minister who cannot support a cabinet decision is supposed to resign; a minister caught in a SCANDAL frequently resigns his seat in the House as well, usually in a huff. Cabinet ministers are also responsible for administering the departments of government and ensuring that their policies are carried out, a task they perform with varying degrees of energy and success. A cabinet minister who is incompetent or unpopular is usually transferred to another portfolio, or dropped from the cabinet altogether (*see*: CORRUPTION, GOSSIP, SCANDAL), and the best ministers move up from minor departments to senior portfolios such as Justice, Finance, and External Affairs, avoiding, if possible, controversial departments such as Immigration and Indian Affairs. Within the cabinet, the powerful Planning and Priorities Committee meets separately to determine policy. A change in ministers is called a cabinet shuffle. In 1867 Canada had a cabinet of thirteen ministers, in 1991 there were thirty-nine, seven of whom were women. For one hundred years the cabinet met in the Privy Council room in the East Block; now it meets on the third floor of the Centre Block. Cabinet ministers are paid more than other members and receive many other PERKS.

Canada

Canada is a constitutional monarchy, a federal state of ten provinces and two territories, where power is shared between provincial governments and the national or federal government (*see*: CONSTITUTION). The provinces, from east to west, are: Newfoundland, Nova Scotia, Prince Edward Island, New Brunswick, Quebec, Ontario, Manitoba, Saskatchewan, Alberta, and British Columbia. Each province is governed by an elected legislature similar to the House of Commons, but no Senate. The two northern territories, the Yukon and the Northwest Territories, have elected councils but do not yet have full self-government. With nearly ten million square kilometres, Canada is the world's second largest country (after Russia) in terms of geography, but with only 27 million people, it is one of the most sparsely populated. The Canadian economy has traditionally been based on the export and refinement of natural resources: oil and gas, grain, timber, minerals, and fish. The name is derived from the Huron-Iroquois word *kanata*, meaning village.

Canada Day

See: JULY 1.

Carillon

Two-thirds of the way up the Peace Tower, hidden behind a stone lattice, the bells of the carillon chime the hours and quarter-hours shown on the tower's illuminated clock face. The four-note Westminster chime is the same as

One of the largest bells in the carillon being removed from its casting mould.

NATIONAL ARCHIVES OF CANADA/PA-43794

The Dominion Carilloneur, Gordon Slater, with two of his bells.

PAUL VON BAICH

Big Ben in London, and the bells' pleasant tones can be heard for miles. The carillon has fifty-three bronze bells ranging in size from 10 pounds (4.5 kg) to 22,400 pounds (10,160 kg). The bells are stationary and are struck by steel clappers manipulated by a complex series of cables and pulleys. Located directly below the bells, the carillon looks like a cross between an organ and a medieval torture chamber. It is played by a system of levers and pedals that requires considerable physical strength, a job to delight the Hunchback of Notre Dame. Every weekday at 12:30 p.m. the Dominion Carillonneur plays a fifteen-minute concert, and on major national holidays and Sunday evenings in the summer he plays a one-hour concert. The music ranges from Handel and Bach to popular folk tunes. Rock and jazz are out: a boppy rhythm is not something bells do well. The carillon was installed in 1927 in honour of Canada's Diamond Jubilee and the largest bell, the one that strikes the hours, was engraved with the name of the current prime minister, William Lyon Mackenzie King, an eccentric spiritualist who communicated with the dead. If something goes wrong with the carillon it is usually King's bell, and King's ghost is believed to haunt the belfry.

Caucus

Every Wednesday morning at 10:00 a.m., members of each political party meet together to thrash out party policy, air their grievances, and assess their performances during the previous week. Closed to the media and the public, caucus meetings are often rowdy and rambunctious, especially if the party is in hot water in the House. Caucus meetings are often the only opportunity MPs have to speak to their party leader, and the leaders use the meetings to bolster their members' spirits and rouse their energies. Parliamentary democracy is not unlike a football game, with rival teams trying to score points and win a victory, and the caucus room is each team's clubhouse.

Centennial Flame

The gas flame burning perpetually in the low fountain at the entrance to Parliament Hill was lit at midnight on New Year's Eve 1966 to commemorate Canada's centennial in 1967. The red granite fountain is embossed

Lit in 1967, the Centennial Flame commemorates Canada's first one hundred years as a nation.

DENIS DREVER / NCC / CCN

with the crests and flowers of the ten provinces and two territories and inscribed with the dates when each province joined Confederation. The fountain is a popular place for visitors to rest and have their pictures taken; the coins thrown into the water are donated to charity.

Centre Block

The largest and most dominant of the buildings on Parliament Hill, the Centre Block symbolizes Parliament to all Canadians. The chamber of the HOUSE OF COMMONS is located in its west wing, the SENATE chamber in its east wing, and the PEACE TOWER rises majestically over its main entrance. The Centre

The Centre Block, with its monumental Peace Tower, is a national symbol familiar to every Canadian.

NATIONAL ARCHIVES OF CANADA / C-5856

Block also houses the SPEAKER's rooms, the LIBRARY OF PARLIAMENT, the Parliamentary DINING ROOM, the private office of the PRIME MINISTER, and the offices of party leaders, many backbenchers, clerks, and staff. The Centre Block is the heart of the Parliamentary mystique, but it is only one of the buildings that form the precinct of the House of Commons. *See also*: ARCHITECTURE, BUILDINGS, FIRE, OFFICES, PRECINCT, STONE CARVING.

Chambers

All Parliamentary debates take place within the chambers of the House of Commons or the Senate. The Commons chamber is eighty-six feet long, fifty-six feet wide, and fifty feet high; the Senate chamber is slightly smaller. The Commons chamber is furnished in moss green; the desks and panelling are carved oak, the curtains rust velvet. The ceiling is linen handpainted in the floral emblems of the provinces, and the official flower of each province and territory is depicted in the stained-glass windows. Carved limestone panels illustrating the Constitution are placed at intervals around the walls; the ornate gilded frieze around the ceiling is plaster moulded into tiny human figures. The cathedral-like ambience of the Commons chamber reflects its origins in St. Stephen's Chapel, Westminister.

The Senate chamber is furnished in dark red with walnut desks and oak panelling; ten large paintings depicting scenes from the First World War decorate the walls. The Senate chamber does not have stained glass windows, but its magnificent gilt ceiling is set with recessed glass panels depicting the emblems of Canada, Great Britain, and France. For years it was believed that the Senate's chandeliers were a gift from the czar of Russia, but they were actually made in Canada. The ambience of the Senate chamber is more intimate and luxurious than the Commons; it does not have lobbies and galleries along each side, and at the north end there is a raised dias with a canopied throne for the monarch or governor general to use at the Opening of Parliament. *See also*: GREEN, HOUSE OF COMMONS, RED, SENATE, STAINED GLASS, STONE CARVINGS.

The colourful Changing of the Guard ceremony on the lawn of Parliament Hill.

PAUL VON BAICH

Changing of the Guard

A colourful military drill based on the ceremony at Buckingham Palace in London, the Changing of the Guard is performed on the lawn of Parliament Hill daily at 10:00 a.m. during the summer months. The student reservists of the Governor General's Foot Guards and Canadian Grenadier Guards look smart in their scarlet tunics and tall bearskin hats and the precision of their manoeuvres is impressive, but the ceremony has no real relationship to Parliament and belongs more appropriately to the governor general's residence, Rideau Hall, where a smaller version of the Changing of the Guard takes place. Led by a colour party and the regimental band, the new guard forms up at the Cartier Square Drill Hall by the Rideau Canal at 9:30 a.m. and marches to Parliament Hill via Laurier, Elgin, and Wellington streets. *See also:* GOVERNOR GENERAL, PARLIAMENT, SECURITY, TOURISTS.

Charter of Rights and Freedoms

Included in the CONSTITUTION Act of 1982, the Charter guarantees every Canadian's right to vote, to enter and leave the country, to move freely within it, and to "life, liberty and security of the person in accordance with the principles of fundamental justice." It also guarantees equality before the law without discrimination based on race, national or ethnic origin, colour, religion, sex, age, or mental or physical disability. It establishes English and French as Canada's two official languages and defines four fundamental freedoms: freedom of conscience and religion; freedom of thought, belief, opinion, and expression; freedom of peaceful assembly; and freedom of association. However, the Charter also states that these rights and freedoms are subject to "reasonable limits prescribed by law." Therefore, the Charter is constantly being challenged in the Supreme Court of Canada, which now has the power to define more precisely the character of Canadian democracy. *See also*: BILL OF RIGHTS.

Civil Service

More than 520,000 civil servants carry out the daily tasks of implementing federal government programs, including the RCMP, the military, and Crown corporations. Canada has many social programs, such as medicare, Canada Pension, and Unemployment Insurance, which require complex administration, as well as a complicated Goods and Services Tax to collect. Civil servants are located in every corner of the country, from meteorologists in the high Arctic to custom's inspectors on the American border and coast-guard patrols miles out to sea. Paid for by taxes and obliged to enforce often unpopular policies, civil servants are a perennial target for public criticism, especially when they go on strike. Politicians regularly promise to reduce or reform the civil service but it mysteriously grows in both size and influence (*see*: BUREAU-CRACY). The highest-ranking civil servant in each department is the deputy minister, who advises his cabinet minister about policy and not infrequently creates it himself.

Cleaners

Like all houses, the Houses of Parliament have to be kept clean, and MPs are not expected to take out their own garbage. Every morning starting at 5:30 a.m. an army of 250 cleaners makes its way through the silent halls and empty offices, mopping, dusting, vacuuming, and emptying wastebaskets into clear plastic garbage bags. Every MP lives in a welter of paper, political souvenirs, and assorted junk, the price of a public life representing thousands of constituents, and because of the confidential nature of an MP's work, the cleaners are not allowed to touch his papers or personal effects: they dust around them. Some MPs are neat as pins, others are slobs. If an MP doesn't want his office cleaned, it won't be cleaned, although the presence of leftover food and hidden snacks creates concern about mice and insects. The cleaners also water the plants, wash coffee mugs, and remove dirty dishes and liquor bottles (*see*: LIQUOR, RESTAURANTS). Occasionally a cleaner will come across an MP asleep on his sofa, often much the worse for wear (*see*: POKER). The cleaner quietly leaves, returning when the MP has gone. The cleaners also dust and vacuum the chambers and the committee rooms, set up chairs and tables for the day's meetings, and mop the marble floors in the corridors with a non-slip wax. By the time the great oak doors swing open at 9:00 a.m. Parliament is as spotless as it can be and the cleaners are heading home. *See also*: OFFICES.

Cleaners work in the early hours of the morning to make sure the Commons chamber is spotless by the time the doors open.

CHARTRAND / CANAPRESS

Clerks

The most invisible, unobtrusive people on Parliament Hill, the clerks are also the most indispensible; without the clerks, both the business of Parliament and the daily routine of the Hill would grind to a halt. The chief clerks of the House of Commons and of the Senate are the senior administrators of Parliament Hill as well as impartial advisers to the Speakers, MPs, and senators. In the chambers of the Commons and the Senate, the Clerk sits at the head of the TABLE, where he is in charge of keeping accurate daily records of proceedings, recording votes, and determining the proper order of business. It is up to the Clerk to ensure that the rules of PROCEDURE are followed in all legislation passed by

Parliament. Bills and motions presented by both the government and private members are approved in advance by the Clerk's office, and in case of disputes on the floor the Clerk provides the SPEAKER with precedents to help him make a ruling. The Clerk also advises MPs and senators on correct behaviour and the intricacies of the legislative system. Powerful and respected, the Clerk also plays a ceremonial role at Parliamentary

The Clerk of the House of Commons, Robert Marleau, sits at the head of the table on the floor of the Commons chamber directly in front of the Speaker, John Fraser.

CANAPRESS

receptions and on state occasions. The Clerk of the Commons, his Deputy and Assistant follow the Speaker in the Speaker's Parade and, like the Speaker, they wear a form of court dress: black suits, white collars with wing tabs, and black gowns. A career as a clerk is a life's calling; students hired out of university can expect to spend ten to fifteen years apprenticing in committees and research libraries before their expertise allows them to sit at the table of the Commons or Senate. Over the years, the clerks' knowledge of the history and drama of Parliament surpasses that of scholars, reporters, and prime ministers.

Colony

Canada was formed by the federation of several British colonies into one nation. One of these original colonies, British Columbia, was located on the West Coast, the others were on the East Coast and along the St. Lawrence River. The oldest of these settlements was established at Quebec City in 1608 as a colony of France. By the eighteenth century, France claimed most of North America, an empire extending as far west as the present Prairie provinces and south to the mouth of the Mississippi River: the state of Louisiana was named for King Louis XIV of France. New France was ruled by a governor and council appointed by the king, and after the British CONQUEST in 1763 the colonial system remained basically the same, although the king changed. Because of the autocratic nature of colonial government, rebellion broke out in both Ontario and Quebec in 1837. The rebellions were suppressed, but reforms were begun in all the colonies which led to responsible government and the formation of Canada in 1867. *See also*: CONFEDERATION, HISTORY.

Committees

Detailed study of proposed legislation is done by MPs and senators in committees. Some committees have so much work to do they are constituted on a permanent basis as standing committees, although their membership changes from session to session. In 1991 there were twenty standing committees, each with between seven and fourteen members. Most MPs belong to more than one committee, including legislative committees set up to examine a particular bill and joint committees with the Senate. Standing committees investigate such important issues as human rights, health and welfare, labour, external affairs, finance, the environment, justice, communications, and culture. They have wide powers to criticize government policy, investigate expenses, and evaluate the performance of government departments; however, since the majority of committee members usually belong to the government party, their recommendations are often uncontentious. As a result committee meetings are rarely covered by the media, although most are open to the public and summon witnesses to appear before them. Committees meet during Parliamentary sessions, and MPs are often absent from debates because they are attending meetings. *See also*: MEMBER OF PARLIAMENT.

Confederation

Canada began as a much smaller nation than it is today. In 1867 only four provinces united to form the Dominion of Canada: Nova Scotia, New Brunswick, Quebec, and Ontario. The largely uninhabited land to the west was known simply as Rupert's Land. In 1869 Canada purchased Rupert's Land north of the forty-ninth parallel from the Hudson's Bay Company, which had been granted a royal charter in 1670 for the purpose of trapping fur (*see*: BEAVER) and in 1870 the province of Manitoba was formed, followed by British Columbia in 1871 and Alberta and Saskatchewan in 1905. Prince Edward Island joined Canada in 1873, but the island of Newfoundland remained a British colony until 1949. *See also*: FATHERS OF CONFEDERATION, HISTORY.

Confederation Hall

See: ROTUNDA.

Conquest

In 1756 war broke out between Great Britain and France. The Seven Years' War involved both nations' colonies in North America; in 1757 the British captured the French fort of Louisbourg at the entrance to the Gulf of St. Lawrence and in

1759 sent a fleet of ships under General James Wolfe up the St. Lawrence to attack Quebec, the capital of New France. High on a cliff above the river, the citadel of Quebec was believed to be impregnable, but Wolfe's soldiers found a path up the rock and engaged the French in a pitched battle on the Plains of Abraham. The French were defeated and their general, the Marquis de Montcalm, mortally wounded; General Wolfe was killed in the battle, but the British captured Quebec. Montreal fell the next year, and when the war ended in 1763 New France became a British possession. The sixty thousand French inhabitants were guaranteed the right to retain their property, their religion, and their civil law; and a unique community of French speaking Roman Catholics took root in Quebec. Canada therefore is a nation of "two founding peoples," although the Native people insist that it is three. *See also*: CONFEDERATION, CONSTITUTION, UNITY.

Constitution

Canada's Constitution has always been a source of dissension and contro- versy. Dividing power between ten provinces, two territories, and a federal government leads to wrangling and jostling for power, especially when one province, Quebec, is predominantly French-speaking, and all are unequal in wealth and population. The Constitution is not one single document, but a series. The most important documents are the Royal Proclamation of 1763 and the BRITISH NORTH AMERICA ACT passed by the British Parliament in 1867. The Constitution is also based on the unwritten conventions and traditions of British Parliamentary democracy; challenges to these laws and conventions are continually being heard by the Supreme Court, and the decisions of the court become part of con- stitutional practice.

Because it was an act of the British Parliament, the BNA Act could only be amended by the British Parliament. In 1982, at the request of the Canadian gov- ernment, the British Parliament relinquished all legislative authority over Canada, and the Constitution Act, 1982, gave Canada its own Constitution. The content remained essentially the same, except a CHARTER OF RIGHTS AND FREEDOMS was added, as well as formulas for amending the Constitution subject to the agreement of the provinces. The province of Quebec did not accept the amending formulas and did not fully agree to the new constitution, which, however, includes Quebec. In 1987, the federal government drafted the Meech Lake accord designed to overcome Quebec's objections, but the accord was not unanimously ratified by the other provinces and failed to be incorporated. *See also*: CONQUEST, PARLIAMENT, UNITY.

Constituencies

Each of the 295 members of Parliament represents a constituency or riding. Constituencies vary in size from densely populated urban neighbourhoods with more than 120,000 voters to vast, sparsely populated regions with 40,000 voters: the entire Yukon Territory elects only one MP. Each MP has a constituency office, paid for by TAXPAYERS, with a small staff to respond to public requests. Most MPs maintain a residence in their constituencies and try to spend weekends and holidays there. Husbands and wives of MPs often remain at home in the constituency and play an active, informal political role. *See also*: ELECTION, PARTIES, SALARIES.

Corruption

Usually associated with graft. Members of Parliament and senators occasionally abuse their power and privileges to make extra money for themselves or to do illegal favours for their friends. Most corruption takes the form of bribes and kickbacks to politicians from private citizens or corporations interested in acquiring government business. A cabinet minister accused of corruption is usually asked to resign. He is then subject to a police investigation and, if the evidence is sufficient, a trial. Corruption usually ends an MP's political career, although he may still be successful in private life, and the SCANDAL may contribute to the defeat of his party at the next election. *See also*: PATRONAGE, PERKS, PRESS GALLERY.

Crown

Canada's status as a constitutional monarchy is symbolized by a crown, and the traditional authority of the queen or king is customarily referred to as "the Crown." In the judicial system, state prosecutors are called "Crown" attorneys and legal actions initiated by the state are referred to as "The Queen [Regina] vs. John Doe." The crown is repeatedly depicted in the decor of the Parliament buildings but its symbolism has been replaced in general use by the word "Canada" and the maple leaf.

D

Daycare

The sound of children's laughter can often be heard behind the austere Confederation Building to the west of Parliament Hill. The House of Commons' daycare centre, Children on the Hill, is located in the basement of the building and a small playground outside the rear entrance. The brainchild of Speaker Jeanne Sauvé in 1982, Children on the Hill offers bilingual (English and

Pre-school children enjoy a game in the yard outside the daycare centre in the Confederation Building.

PAUL VON BAICH

French) non-profit daycare for the pre-school children of MPs, senators, House of Commons' staff, and private citizens who can get on the waiting list for the thirty-five places. Although most MPs are middle-aged, some of them have young families, and an increasing number of women with children are working on Parliament Hill.

Debate

Most of the time of the House of Commons is spent debating the bills placed before it. Debate takes place on the Speech from the Throne (*see:* OPENING) and on the second and third reading of every BILL as well as on motions and amendments. Debate is initiated by a cabinet minister or MP who introduces a bill, and opposition critics are chosen by their parties to attempt to amend, delay, or defeat the bill. An MP who wishes to enter a debate jumps to his feet when the previous MP sits down and tries to catch the eye of the Speaker to be recognized. Each speaker is limited to twenty minutes; the prime minister and the leader of the Opposition are allowed forty. Debate is conducted according to strict rules, and an MP who breaks those rules will be asked by the Speaker to sit down or may be expelled from the chamber (*see:* NAMING, UNPARLIAMENTARY). In debate, MPs never address each other directly or call each other by name. They direct their remarks to the Speaker with the phrase "Mr. Speaker" or "Madame Speaker," and refer to their opponent across the floor as "my honourable friend" or "the honourable member from Winnipeg North" or "the honourable member opposite," often with exaggerated politeness or sarcasm.

Members of Parliament used to be admired for their skills in debate, but the time limits now placed on debates make oratorical flourishes impossible, and MPs are no longer elected for their speaking ability. A debate requires a quorum of only twenty members to be present, and the House is frequently virtually empty. MPs can follow the debate on television in their offices, or devote the time to work they consider more important. Debates are generally considered too boring and repetitious to be reported by the media, and sometimes an MP will get so discouraged by an empty House and his own rhetoric he will shut up and sit down in the middle of his speech. If the government feels debate has gone on too long and wants to push its legislation through the House, it moves a motion of *closure* that terminates debate at a specified hour. Closure is an unpopular tactic that makes the government appear to be dictatorial. *See also*: HECKLING, QUESTION PERIOD, SPEAKER.

Decorum

When a member of Parliament enters the chamber of the House he nods or bows slightly to the SPEAKER, a legacy of the days when the Speaker sat in front of the altar in St. Stephen's Chapel, Westminster. MPs are expected to behave towards each other with courtesy, however violent their private feelings, and to honour the traditions of the House. Dress must be conservative, contempory clothing, interpreted as a jacket and tie for men and a suit or dress for women: blue jeans, shorts, rolled shirtsleeves, and turtlenecks are frowned on, although MPs of both sexes often wear odd-looking clothes. Women MPs may wear pant suits, but few do. Some MPs used to wear their hats in the chamber, a custom that disappeared along with chewing tobacco and spitoons, and most women MPs have shunned hats. No MP may speak wearing a hat. Smoking used to be allowed in the lobbies behind the curtains, as well as in the corridors and the committee rooms, but now it is banned (*see*: FIRE). MPs are requested not to sleep, read newspapers, write letters, or talk to each other during debate, but this request is often ignored. Eating in the chamber is forbidden, and MPs who appear drunk or disorderly are usually hustled away by the party WHIP. The Speaker can punish MPs who offend decorum by refusing to recognize them in debate. Behaviour in the chamber today is staid compared to the nineteenth century, when MPs hurled books, papers, and abuse at each other and sometimes wrestled each other to the ground. *See also*: HECKLING, LIQUOR.

Defeat

The government can be defeated in the House of Commons on a procedural matter or a minor bill without losing the general confidence of the House, but if it fails to win a vote on a motion it considers one of confidence, the PRIME

MINISTER may ask the governor general to call an election, or he may resign to permit the OPPOSITION to form a government. Defeat can come suddenly and unexpectedly for both governments and MPs. Once defeated, few MPs seek re election. *See also*: DEMOCRACY, ELECTION, GOVERNOR GENERAL, VOTE.

Democracy

Derived from the Greek words "demo," for people, and "kratia," meaning state, the democratic system dates back to the city state of ancient Athens, where leaders were chosen by lot but policies were debated by citizens gathered in the public square. The communities were small, and women and slaves could not vote, but politicians had to be leather-lunged orators with skills to charm the mob if they wanted to achieve power, and power ultimately rested with the majority of the people. During the eighteenth century in England, a revival of interest in Greek culture helped to tilt the balance of political power in favour of the people, or commoners, and away from the hereditary titles of kings and lords.

Demonstration

In the tradition of the English village common or central square, the grounds of Parliament Hill are open to the public, although the gardeners prefer that people don't litter or walk on the grass. The Hill is an ideal place for demonstrations because it is public, it holds a lot of people, and it is easy for demonstrators to confront the prime minister as he tries to get into the House. Demonstrations can be very large, bringing hundreds of thousands of protestors from across the country, or they can consist of only one person with a sign walking up and down. The right to demonstrate on Parliament Hill is considered sacred in Canada and all attempts to ban demonstrations have failed. The RCMP keeps demonstrators away from the doors and will arrest noisy and persistent demonstrators and those whose behaviour is violent or threatening. *See also*: HISTORY, LANDSCAPING, SECURITY.

ice Alliance, on strike against the government, parade on

rner on the sixth floor of the Centre Block, the
is one of the most beautiful rooms on Parliament
Hill. Its tall windows give a spectacular view of the Ottawa River and the
Chaudière Falls and the tables provide a close-up look at famous political person-
alities. The ambience of the dining room, which is decorated in warm shades of
peach and mahogany, is relaxed and non-partisan: the tablecloths are snowy, the
waitresses motherly, and the gourmet meals relatively inexpensive (*see*: PERKS).
MPs who have just been yelling at each other in the House can be found laughing
together over dinner or speculating about the political alignments at adjoining
tables. The dining room is divided into clearly defined political territories. The
alcove immediately to the left of the door is reserved for the prime minister, the

alcove to the right for senators. Each major political party has an alcove to itself where its members can eat together in relative privacy. MPs who wish to be seen and probably heard sit in the centre of the room under the frosted domed skylights – the skylights are said to refract conversations to the farthest corners of the room – and the tables at the back are for those who prefer to be alone. The dining room is open for lunch from 12 noon until 2:30 p.m., Monday to Friday, and for dinner from 6:00 p.m. until 9:00 p.m., Monday to Thursday. It is reserved exclusively for MPs, senators, senior civil servants, and members of the press gallery, however it is a popular place to bring guests. *See also*: GOSSIP, KITCHENS, RESTAURANTS.

E

East Block

Located to the east of the Centre Block, the East Block is the oldest and most historic part of the Parliamentary PRECINCT. Designed in the Gothic Revival style by the architectural firm of Stent and Laver, the East Block is built of sandstone quarried in nearby Nepean, with red sandstone from New York state trimming the doors and windows. Construction on the East Block began in 1860, and it was intended to house the departments of Justice, Finance, and Agriculture as well as the offices of senior ministers, the governor general, and the cabinet or Privy Council room. Equipped with central heat, gas lighting, and running water, the East Block was considered very modern for its time, but wood-burning fireplaces had to be used to keep the offices warm in winter, and gas was replaced by electricity before 1900. Until the telephone arrived on the Hill in 1877, ministers and staff communicated by handwritten notes delivered by messengers who were summoned by battery-operated electric bells, a practice some MPs and senators continue to this day.

Canada was a small nation of less than four million people when the East Block was built, and nobody foresaw the enormous increase in government the next hundred years would bring. Parliament sat for only four months of the year. MPs were paid a modest fee or indemnity to compensate them for their time away from their farms or jobs, and departments were run by clerks who worked from 10:00 a.m. to 4:00 p.m. with two hours off for lunch: one civil servant regularly enjoyed a noonday swim in the attic water tank that fed the plumbing system. Government was highly informal: until 1940 the cabinet kept no agenda and no

The brand new East Block in 1866. The governor general had a private office which he entered through the small portico in the centre of the west wall.

record of its deliberations, and the cabinet room was equipped with a cupboard that concealed an ample supply of sherry, port, brandy, ale, and whisky.

The cabinet met in Room 235 of the East Block until the building was closed for renovations in 1976, and many political dramas have played themselves out in that quiet, secluded room. One civil servant committed suicide in his East Block office, and a disgruntled visitor shot himself in the office of the justice minister. From 1867 until 1976 the prime minister had his office in the East Block, first in Room 201 and later in Room 221 in the northeast corner near the Centre Block; in 1870 Sir John A. Macdonald suffered an attack of gallstones in his office and lay on the couch for days until he was strong enough to be carried to the Speaker's apartments. Now the prime minister has two offices, one in the Centre Block and another across Wellington Street in the Langevin building, which also houses his staff (*see*: PMO). The governor general's office, directly above his private entrance beneath the west portico, was closed in 1942; the prime minister now meets the governor general at his residence, Rideau Hall.

An elevator was installed in the East Block in 1908 and a north wing added in 1910. Between 1976 and 1983, $15 million was spent restoring and renovating the original building. An effort was made to maintain some of the original nineteenth-century style of the interior: the halls are painted dark yellow and old-fashioned ornamental light fixtures cast a dull Dickensian glow. Four of the offices, including those used by the first prime ministers, and the cabinet room have been restored to their original Victorian splendour and are open to public tours on weekends. The rest of the building is now occupied by cabinet ministers and senators and is restricted to the public. *See also*: ARCHITECTURE, BUILD-INGS, RENOVATION, TOURS.

Election

A federal election must be held every five years, although elections are usually more frequent. The prime minister may call an election because his government has lost a vote in the House, or because he thinks he can improve his majority, or because an issue has arisen on which he wants popular support. An unexpected election is called a snap election. An election campaign lasts sixty days and costs the political parties millions of dollars. Most MPs campaign in their own constituencies, although the party leaders fly around the country and appear frequently on radio and television. An MP is expected to advocate party policy and support his leader, but if the party is unpopular he may run a more independent campaign. A political party runs one candidate in each constituency, and there are usually at least three or four parties contesting every seat. All candidates adopt the same tactics to get elected: advertising, public meetings, hand-shaking, door-knocking, and media interviews. Elections are unpredictable and exhausting. Candidates campaign twelve to eighteen hours a day, often to face humiliating defeat: a Canadian MP serves an average of only seven years. If an MP dies or resigns before a general election, the prime minister may call a by-election to fill his vacant seat. If the government is unpopular, the prime minister is often unwilling to run the risk of losing the seat, and several seats may remain vacant until the next general election. Seats are distributed proportionally according to population: Newfoundland, seven; Prince Edward Island, four; Nova Scotia, eleven; New Brunswick, ten; Quebec, seventy-five; Ontario, ninety-nine; Manitoba, fourteen; Saskatchewan, fourteen; Alberta, twenty-six; British Columbia, thirty-two; Yukon, one; Northwest Territories, two. This regional imbalance weights power heavily in favour of Ontario and Quebec, and causes chronic unhappiness in the West and the Atlantic provinces, where voters feel unable to influence national policy. *See also*: GOVERNMENT, GOVERNOR GENERAL, MEMBER OF PARLIAMENT, PARTIES, PRIME MINISTER, VOTERS.

English

One of Canada's two official languages, spoken in the House of Commons, the Senate, and the civil service. The other is FRENCH. Simultaneous translation is provided for MPs and senators who are not bilingual: politicians wearing electronic buttons in their ears are not listening to the radio. All federal government services are available in both official languages throughout the country. *See also*: UNITY.

Fathers of Confederation

Canada's first prime minister, Sir John A. Macdonald, and the politicians who negotiated the federation of the original colonies into the Dominion of Canada in 1867 are known as the Fathers of Confederation. Joey Smallwood, the premier of Newfoundland when it joined Canada in 1949, was also a Father. *See*: CONFEDERATION.

The Fathers of Confederation looking very solemn and patriarchal.

NATIONAL ARCHIVES OF CANADA/C-6350

Filibuster

Senators who object strongly to proposed legislation will sometimes try to "talk it out" by speaking for hours or days without stopping; in 1990 senators brought sleeping bags into their offices in an unsuccessful attempt to filibuster a government taxation bill. Senators are free to speak on any topic of their choice for as long as they like, but in the Commons speeches are limited to twenty minutes and the Speaker can cut short an MP who is repetitious or irrelevant. MPs use procedural tactics instead to delay unpopular legislation in the hope the session will end before it comes to a vote. *See also*: PROCEDURE, SENATE.

Fire

The House of Commons was sitting late on the bitterly cold night of February 3, 1916. At 8:50 p.m. an MP was browsing through newspapers in the READING ROOM when he felt intense heat and noticed that a pile of papers was smouldering. He rushed out to alert a guard, and when they returned moments later the Reading Room was engulfed in smoke and flames. Licking along the dry, varnished wood, the fire raced through the corridors of the Centre Block and thick smoke belched into the Commons chamber. "Get out quickly!" the doorkeeper shouted. MPs ran out into the freezing night without hats or coats. Some tried to salvage furniture and documents, but the flames spread too rapidly, and two young women, guests of the Speaker, who returned for their coats, perished. Just after 10:00 p.m. a series of explosions raised the roof and

The gutted ruin of the Centre Block the morning after the fire on February 3, 1916. Frozen water from the small steam fire engines has formed a crust of ice on the charred façade.

NATIONAL ARCHIVES OF CANADA / RD-243

The fire spread so quickly that almost nothing could be saved. Seven people trapped inside were burned to death.

NATIONAL ARCHIVES OF CANADA / RD-244

sent flames a hundred feet into the air. As the fire crept higher and higher, the bell in the clock tower solemnly tolled the hour. At midnight it tolled eleven times then crashed to the ground.

One MP, B. B. Law of Yarmouth, Nova Scotia, was killed in the fire, and several people were badly burned. Two guards and two staff members also lost their lives. Canada was at war with Germany, and it was speculated that the fire was the work of German terrorists, but no evidence of sabotage was found. An investigation was inconclusive, but it was generally believed the fire was started accidentally by a careless smoker in the Reading Room. Fortunately a guard closed the steel door leading to the LIBRARY OF PARLIAMENT and while blackened by smoke on the outside, the Library remained unharmed until 1952 when a fire in the roof caused severe damage. Temporary accomodation for the Commons and the Senate was set up in the Victoria Museum, and Parliament met there until the new Centre Block was completed in 1920. *See also*: ARCHITECTURE, BUILDINGS, PORTRAITS.

Fitness

Some MPs are fat, some are lean, but because of the stressful and sedentary nature of their work they worry about their health. The Hill provides resident nurses, and MPs get priority treatment at an Ottawa military hospital, but there is no swimming pool (*see*: 24 SUSSEX DRIVE) or health club. A small room in the

Confederation Building provides exercise equipment, a sauna, and the services of a masseur, but otherwise MPs and senators are expected to walk, run, skate, or ski on their own. Their health is remarkably good. Few MPs die in office, and so far prime ministers have lived to a ripe old age: the single exception is Sir John Thompson who died in 1894 of a cerebral hemorrhage at the age of forty-nine.

Flag

The Canadian flag, a red maple leaf on a white background with a red border on either side, was adopted in 1965 after years of controversy over the design and whether a new flag was needed at all; Canada's previous flag was the British Red Ensign, a red background with a small Union Jack in the upper left corner and the shield of Canada to the right of centre. The red maple leaf on Canada's flag is now recognized internationally as Canada's symbol. The flag on the Peace Tower measures fifteen feet by seven-and-a-half feet; it flies day and night and is replaced once a month.

Fossils

The freckled Tyndall limestone from Manitoba lining the walls, arches, and ceilings of the corridors in the Centre Block was once the mud bottom of prehistoric Lake Agassiz. The rocks are embedded with the fossils of early plant and animal life, and the fossils form a natural counterpart to the sculpted shapes of plants, fish, and crustaceans that adorn the arches of the FOYERS, ROTUNDA, and HALL OF HONOUR. *See also*: SENATE, STONE CARVINGS.

Foyer

Members of Parliament usually enter the Centre Block through the oak doors to the west of the main entrance. Inside, a marble staircase leads to the foyer of the Commons chamber, a two-storey rectangular room where MPs gather on their way into the chamber. MPs enter the chamber through doors on either side that lead to the curtained LOBBIES and their desks; only the Speaker's Parade uses the main doors, which are closed when the House is not sitting.

A view from the gallery above the House of Commons foyer on budget night. The foyer is a popular place for the media to grab a member of Parliament as he leaves or enters the Commons chamber.
BREGG / CANAPRESS

Illuminated by an etched-glass skylight, the foyer is surrounded by a gallery leading to the offices of the prime minister and the government House leader, who descend by a narrow stone staircase on the west wall. The foyer is open to guided tours, and when the House of Commons is sitting it is often crowded with MPs, aides, and reporters (*see*: SCRUM). Portraits of past prime ministers line the walls, and the foyer is a showplace for the work of the Commons' stone carvers: its highlight is a frieze by Eleanor Milne depicting Canadian history from the Stone Age until the arrival of the United Empire Loyalists after the American Revolution in 1776. The Senate foyer is entered through matching doors in the east wing, and the marble staircase to the Senate is more monumental. Portraits of British kings and queens line the walls of the Senate foyer and the carved heads of former monarchs peer down from the stone arches. *See also*: CHAMBER, PORTRAITS, STAINED GLASS, STONE CARVING, TOURS.

French

One of Canada's two official languages spoken in the House of Commons, the Senate, and the civil service. *See also*: ENGLISH.

French Fries

Canada's unofficial national dish and Ottawa's favourite food. Finger-size sliced potatoes deep-fried in fat, french fries are served with salt, vinegar, ketchup, gravy, onions, cheese curds, or "the works." Fries are also known as chips or *poutine*. *See also*: FITNESS, KITCHENS, RESTAURANTS.

F̶urniture

...of Parliament were equipped with a desk in the ...peg, a hat box, and a box of stationery. That was ...amber, MPs spent their time in the lobbies, the ...smoking rooms, or the saloon. The first offices in ...tan: an oak desk, a filing cabinet, a few straight-...rs were linoleum and the windows had venetian

armchairs, and buffalo hides on a bare plank floor.

FRANK C. TYRRELL/NATIONAL ARCHIVES OF CANADA/C-003353

blinds: an MP who hung curtains in the 1960s created a sensation. MPs are now provided with comfortable sofas and armchairs, but their taste is expected to be practical and inexpensive: no antiques, expensive art, or Oriental carpets. Furniture is stored in government warehouses and built or re-upholstered in a basement workroom in the Wellington Block where carpenters repair broken chairs, cabinet makers build shelving, and refinishers restore damaged woodwork. The House will also frame an MP's pictures or posters. The changing population on the Hill and the heavy wear-and-tear on furniture create a steady demand, although only the prime minister gets customized cabinetry to conceal his video system and hotline telephones. In the course of successive RENOVATIONS, most of the original furnishings have unfortunately been destroyed, discarded, or carted away. *See also*: INTERIOR DESIGN, OFFICES.

G

Galleries

The chamber of the House of Commons is surrounded by public galleries. Two members' galleries run along the sides of the chamber, overlooking the floor of the House. Admittance to these galleries is restricted to guests of MPs, and

How many people does it take to change a light bulb in the House of Commons?

CANAPRESS

signed passes are issued on a daily basis. Guests are shown into the gallery facing the host MP's seat: guests of the government sit above the opposition parties so they have a clear view of the government benches, guests of the opposition sit on the government side. The members' galleries contain sections reserved for guests of the prime minister, the Speaker, and the diplomatic corps. The PRESS GALLERY is located directly above the Speaker's chair. The gallery is too small to accomodate all the media, and reporters usually watch the proceedings on TELEVISION. The public galleries are at either end of the Commons chamber. Access to the public galleries is available on a first-come basis, and during controversial debates visitors will line up far in advance. Coats, bags, tape recorders, and cameras are not permitted in the galleries. Visitors are expected to be quiet and not wave, applaud, or comment on the debate. This rule is not always obeyed (*see*: STRANGERS). *See also*: PRESS GALLERY, QUESTION PERIOD, SECURITY.

Gargoyles

Among the most striking features of the Peace Tower are the four large stone gargoyles that snarl or smirk from the corners below the clock face. Originally created as downspouts to carry water away from the walls, gargoyles are characteristic of the imaginative and mythological designs of Gothic architecture. *See also*: ARCHITECTURE, GROTESQUE, STONE CARVING.

A gargoyle at prayer on the Peace Tower.

CHRIS LUND/NATIONAL ARCHIVES OF CANADA / PA-185326

Gossip

Two or more people seen together on Parliament Hill are probably gossiping. With 295 MPs and 104 senators sharing cramped space in a competitive atmosphere, the Hill is in a constant tizzy of rumour and speculation. Information is power, and no politician survives unless he keeps abreast of the personal feuds and changing alliances within his own party as well as among his opponents. An MP's ears are always cocked for information he might use against an opponent (*see*: SCANDAL), and he is eager to publicize his own achievements. One of the functions of an AIDE is to pick up and circulate gossip useful to his MP (*see*: PRESS GALLERY). True or false, parliamentary gossip is always scandalous, shocking, and unprintable.

Government:

The political party that wins more than half the 295 seats in the House of Commons forms a *majority* government. A party that wins fewer than half the seats may form a *minority* government with the support of one or more of the smaller parties. A government with a comfortable majority is rarely defeated in the House (*see*: WHIP) and can govern for up to five years without an election. A minority government enables small parties to force legislation favourable to their interests in exchange for their unpredictable support; many of the most important and progressive new programs in Canadian history have been passed by minority governments. *See also*: CABINET, ELECTION, PRIME MINISTER, SENATE.

Governor General

The head of state and the representative of the Crown, the governor general performs in Canada the functions of the king or queen in Great Britain. These duties are largely symbolic and ceremonial, but the governor general retains the right to discuss policy with the prime minister, to offer advice and to warn against possible danger to the nation. Discussions with the prime minister are confidential. The governor general must publicly express no political opinions and take

The governor general and his wife, Earl and Countess Grey, receive the debutants of 1907 in the Senate chamber following the Opening of Parliament.

NATIONAL ARCHIVES OF CANADA / C-14131

no part in partisan political activity, but he must make sure there is always a government in office. The governor general opens a new session of Parliament by reading the Speech from the Throne (*see*: OPENING) and must sign all bills before they become law (*see*: ROYAL ASSENT). It is the governor general who calls on the leader of a party to form a government, and the prime minister must obtain the governor general's permission before calling an election. The governor general receives foreign ambassadors and heads of state and represents Canada abroad, patronizes worthy causes, and speaks to schools and clubs across the country. He is Commander-in-Chief of the armed forces and Chief Companion of the Order of Canada.

The governor general is appointed by the prime minister for an indefinite term that usually lasts five to seven years, and he remains in office even if the government changes. Canada's first governors general were British aristocrats appointed by the British monarch, including several members of the royal family, but since 1952 the governor general has been a Canadian and a commoner. One woman, Jeanne Sauvé, served as governor general from 1984 to 1990. Expected to behave with dignity, the governor general occasionally wears military or court uniform on state occasions. The original court uniform, a cocked hat with a white plume, navy tunic, breeches, and white silk stockings, was retired by Governor General Jules Leger in favour of a black morning coat and striped trousers, however some governors general have designed their own uniforms and Madame Sauvé wore flowing formal gowns of silk and velvet. The governor general has two official residences, RIDEAU HALL at the end of Sussex Drive in Ottawa and La Citadelle in Quebec City. The grounds of Rideau Hall are open to the general public year-round and are a popular place for walks and cricket; the public rooms in the residence are open to associations, educational organizations, and social clubs upon request. Every New Year's Day the governor general holds an open house or *levée* to which the public is invited, and in June he throws a garden party on the grounds. Canada's most prestigious literary prizes, the Governor General's Literary Awards, were established in 1936 by Lord Tweedsmuir, the famous British novelist John Buchan. Governor General Lord Grey donated the Grey Cup for football in 1909 and Lord Stanley the Stanley Cup for hockey in 1893.

Graft

See: CORRUPTION.

Green

The House of Commons is traditionally decorated in green, the Senate in RED. Red is a royal colour, in keeping with the Senate's origins in the House of Lords, but the origins of the Commons' green are more obscure. It may also be a royal tradition: green was the favourite colour of the thirteenth-century

English king Henry III, and when the commoners were summoned to meet in his palace at Westminster, they met in rooms painted in shades of green. The green of the Commons is a muted, mossy shade. In 1990, the Commons adopted a "green" policy of energy conservation and recycling.

Grotesque

Medieval artisans were fond of including caricatures in their work, and many of the carved faces on Parliament Hill have a grotesquely exaggerated appearance. Twelve grimmacing musicians cavort on the Peace Tower above the CARILLON, and some of the carved heads inside have rude and leering expressions not inappropriate to Parliament. The artisans liked to include their own portraits as well: the heads of the first stone carvers adorn the Senate foyer and the grotesque busts of Thomas Fuller and John A. Pearson, the architects of the first and second Centre Blocks, protrude from the main walls on either side of the Peace Tower. *See also*: STONE CARVING.

One of the hundreds of fantastic grotesques adorning the walls and arches of the Centre Block.

CHRIS LUND/NATIONAL ARCHIVES OF CANADA / PA-185328

Guides

Parliament employs between thirty and forty guides full time in the summer months and part time during the winter. The guides are all university students recruited from across Canada. Guides must be fluent in both English and French and able to answer a myriad of questions about Canadian politics and history. The guides lead brief tours of the principal public areas of the Centre Block and the historic offices of the East Block. *See also:* TOURS.

Hall of Honour

The wide arched passageway running north from the ROTUNDA of the Centre Block to the LIBRARY OF PARLIAMENT is called the Hall of Honour. The walls contain memorials to the men and women killed in the FIRE of 1916 and to Canadian nurses killed in the First World War. Short hallways on either side lead to large committee rooms and the Speaker's corridor intersects in front of the Library doors; at the beginning of every day's sitting of the

The gothic arches of the Hall of Honour.

PAUL VON BAICH

House of Commons, the Speaker's Parade makes its way briskly along the Hall of Honour towards the Commons chamber. Plans originally called for the Hall of Honour to be lined with statues and memorials to prominent citizens, but the crowds of people constantly using the hall have made it impractical.

Hansard

Named after Luke Hansard, the first printer to the British House of Commons in the eighteenth-century, Hansard is the verbatim printed record of all Senate debates, House of Commons' debates and Question Periods. Until recently debates were recorded by relays of shorthand reporters seated on the floor of

A Hansard employee waits to transcribe a cassette tape into a computer terminal.

MONE CHENG PHOTOGRAPHY STUDIO

the chamber, but now the two Hansard floor monitors simply note interruptions and other disturbances in the chamber; the speeches are recorded on tape in a room across the hall. Each five-minute tape is then transcribed into a computer, and an editor goes through the text to eliminate false starts, ums, ahs, and gibberish. The challenge of the Hansard editors is to shape each member's spoken rhetoric into a comprehensible printed document that reflects the MP's intent and personality. Heckling, admonitions, and other interruptions recorded by the monitors are integrated into the Hansard record (*see*: OH! OH!). The edited transcript is printed out and sent to the MP for his approval; he has no more than three hours to make corrections. While mispronunciations and garbled syntax may be corrected, an editor will not accept corrections that alter or censor the meaning of the speech. The corrections are entered in the computer and the French is translated into English and vice versa. Overnight the day's complete Hansard is assembled electronically and printed at the QUEEN'S PRINTER: it is supposed to be on every member's desk by nine the next morning. Hansard is subscribed to by newspapers and libraries, where it is read by many voters. *See also*: TELEVISION.

Hear, Hear!

When an MP makes a particularly brilliant, witty, or effective remark, his colleagues will shout "Hear, hear!" and applaud, laugh, or bang their desks. Short for "Hear him!" or "Listen up!" the shouts are usually drowned out by groans and HECKLING from the other side.

Heckling

MPs often interrupt an opponent's speech by laughing, hooting, or shouting insults. Heckling is usually done with good humour to test a politician's wits, but if the hecklers become disorderly and the noise deafening, the Speaker will rise and, if necessary, eject the hecklers from the House. *See also*: NAMING, OH, OH!, QUESTION PERIOD, UNPARLIAMENTARY.

Hill

Situated on a bluff overlooking the Ottawa River once called Barracks Hill, the Parliament Buildings and grounds are commonly referred to as the Hill. In 1802 the Hill was part of a land grant awarded by the British governor to a Loyalist who had fought on the British side in the American Revolution. As farm or timber land it was worthless, and in 1823 the governor, Lord Dalhousie, bought it back for 750 pounds sterling with an eye to building a fort. When the British began constructing the Rideau Canal to link the Ottawa River with the Great Lakes in 1826, barracks to house the Royal Miners and Sappers were built on the Hill and surrounded by a stockade. The canal was completed in 1832, and in 1856 the small garrison of British troops left for the Crimean War. The fact that the Crown already owned the Hill probably played a role in persuading Queen Victoria to choose Ottawa as the site for Canada's capital in 1858. *See also*: LANDSCAPING, PRECINCT.

History

Canada's Parliament grew out of the legislative assemblies elected in the eighteenth-century British colonies to advise the governor and his executive council. The governor was appointed by the British king, and usually served only a brief time, but the council could remain in power for generations. As historian Peter Waite puts it: "The Executive Council of Nova Scotia was based on four or five families and their intermarriages. The problem was not that such oligarchies were stupid or ineffective; they were generally all too efficient – at looking after friends and relatives and using the government, when it suited them, for their own purposes. They had learned how to recruit able young men to their ranks by marrying off their daughters to bright aspirants on the prowl for place, preferment and patronage." In Upper Canada, now Ontario, the council was known as the "Family Compact." Able to grant themselves powerful positions and large tracts of land, these colonial aristocrats aroused the anger of the farmers and tradesmen, who demanded the right to govern themselves. In

Quebec, or Lower Canada, the French-speaking inhabitants deeply resented being governed by English rulers. In 1837, rebellion broke out in both Upper and Lower Canada. The rebellions were crushed, but in an attempt at reform the two colonies were united into the Province of Canada. Montreal was chosen as the capital, and the legislative assembly met in the Ste-Anne Market. Rivalry between the French Catholics and British Protestants made the assemblies bitter and violent, and in 1849 the Ste-Anne Market was burned to the ground by a British mob. For the next ten years, Canada's Parliament was homeless, alternating every two years between Toronto and Quebec City, unable to find a location that would satisfy both French and English. In 1857 the assembly petitioned Queen Victoria to choose a site, and in 1858 the Queen selected Ottawa.

The Province of Canada now had more than two million people, and the emergence of Conservative and Reform parties in the British tradition, uniting French and British members in common political causes, made the province capable of running its own affairs. The election of Reform governments in Nova Scotia and the Province of Canada in 1848 destroyed the Family Compacts and the veto power of the British governors, and in 1860 the outbreak of the American Civil War encouraged Canadians to bury their differences of race, language, and religion in the interest of self-preservation: a war between Britain and the Union states could result in Canada being ceded to the Americans, and however different the French and British Canadians were in other ways, they were not republicans. As a collection of separate, small colonies, British North America was weak and disorganized; between 1864 and Confederation in 1867 the leading colonial politicians established the groundwork for a self-sufficient, self-governing nation, the Dominion of Canada, that entrenched the principles of British parliamentary government in North America.

Hours

The hours the House of Commons sits vary each day of the week: Mondays from 11:00 a.m. to 6:00 p.m; Tuesdays and Thursdays from 10:00 a.m. to 6:00 p.m.; Wednesdays from 2:00 p.m. to 8:00 p.m.; and Fridays from 10:00

a.m. to 4:00 p.m. The staggered hours make it possible for all parties to hold caucus meetings on Wednesday mornings and allow MPs who have long distances to travel to spend longer weekends in their constituencies.

House of Commons

Within Canada's multi-level political system, ultimate power rests with the House of Commons: only the Commons may introduce federal financial legislation and set the national budget. Other legislation may be initiated by the Commons or the SENATE, and it becomes law when passed by both houses. While the governor general may advise the prime minister and must sign all acts

The Commons chamber in the original Centre Block was spartan and simple. The desks were arranged across the width of the room. The Bar can be seen on the right, the Speaker's chair on the left.

of Parliament, neither he nor the Queen has the power to alter or veto the bills they approve. Members of Parliament are elected to the House of Commons at least once every five years and they represent all parts of the country in proportion to population. *See also*: ELEC-TION, GOVERNMENT.

The chamber in 1991 with the House of Commons in session.

MONE CHENG PHOTOGRAPHY STUDIO

House of Lords

Unlike Great Britain, Canada does not have a hereditary aristocracy and therefore no House of Lords. In the nineteenth-century it was customary for Canadian prime ministers to be knighted by Queen Victoria as a mark of honour, although a Liberal, Alexander Mackenzie, twice refused. The last prime minister to accept a knighthood was Sir Robert Borden in 1911, and the last Canadian citizens were knighted in 1935. One former prime minister, R. B. Bennett, entered the British House of Lords as Viscount Bennett in 1940 and a prime minister's wife, Agnes Macdonald, became Baroness Macdonald of Earnscliffe after Sir John A. Macdonald's death in 1891. Canadians may still become lords or peers if they become British citizens. In 1977 Canada established a civilian order of merit, the Order of Canada, which carries no hereditary or political obligations. *See also*: SENATE.

House Leader

Each party in the House of Commons chooses one MP as its House Leader. His job is to negotiate the Commons' timetable with his counterparts; to determine which MPs will speak during QUESTION PERIOD; to supervise the work of the party WHIP; and to be the House tactician for his caucus. The government House Leader is invariably a cabinet member, given the honorific title of president of the PRIVY COUNCIL.

Housekeeping

See: BUDGET, CLEANERS, STAFF.

Hull

Directly across the Ottawa River from the Parliament buildings, the city of Hull is the site of Canada's national museum, the Museum of Civilization, and a government office complex. French-speaking and located in the province of Quebec, Hull is historically known as the place Ottawa goes to have fun. With its French ambience, anonymity, and late-night liquor laws, Hull traditionally provided weekend solace for Quebec MPs who couldn't make the train to Montreal. Going "over to Hull" is a familiar cry on Parliament Hill. *See also*: LIQUOR, SCANDAL.

I

Independent

MPs who are affiliated with no party organization are Independents. An MP who disagrees with his party's policy may sit as an Independent until he joins another party or leaves politics. Without the financial resources of a party organization or the strength of numbers, an Independent's political career tends to be solitary and short.

Information

The Public Information Office is the central source for information about all aspects of the House of Commons; the Senate Information Office answers questions about the Senate. Both offices can be contacted by mail, phone, and fax. During the summer an "Infotent" is erected on the grounds between the East Block and the Centre Block, and a multitude of questions are answered in the Visitor Centre run by the National Capital Commission at the corner of Metcalfe and Wellington streets. *See also*: TOURISTS, TOURS.

Interns

In 1965 the Canadian Political Science Association established a program to assign ten university graduates to members of Parliament for a ten-month period. Each intern spends five months with a government MP, five months with an opposition MP. The interns follow the instructions of their MPs, and their tasks may include everything from research and speech-writing to stuffing envelopes. Financed by private donors and administered by Carleton University in Ottawa, the intern program is intended to assist MPs and to give young people who have a theoretical knowledge of politics some hands-on experience with how the parliamentary system actually works.

Interior Decorating

The House of Commons has its own interior designer who assists the MPs in choosing appropriate colours and fabrics for their offices. MPs' offices were originally painted drab institutional colours but now an MP is allowed to express his own taste, within limits. Passion-pink walls are frowned on, as are eccentric patterns and pale shades that require constant cleaning. Because of wear and tear, fabrics have to be durable and resistant to soiling. New offices are colour co-ordinated in muted shades with wall-to-wall carpeting, but some veteran MPs have kept their offices exactly as they were twenty or thirty years ago. Cabinet ministers are allowed more expensive furnishings than private members (*see:* PERKS). MPs may redecorate after each election, and when elections are frequent and MPs constantly changing, the House is in a flurry of plastering and painting. *See also:* FURNITURE, OFFICES, RENOVATION.

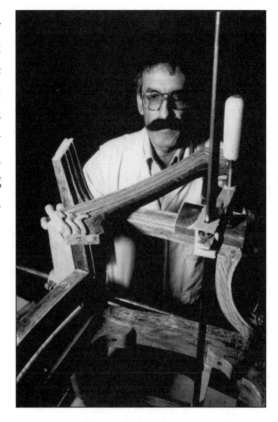

Politics isn't the only craft practised on Parliament Hill; upholstery is important, too.

PAUL VON BAICH

J

Journals

Clerks at the Table of the House of Commons keep a daily record of all Votes and Proceedings that take place during the course of a session. Like HANSARD, the Votes and Proceedings are printed overnight and distributed to MPs the next morning with the ORDERS OF THE DAY. At the end of every session, the daily records are compiled into a journal that provides a complete record of the work of the House.

July 1

Canada Day, commemorating Canada's "birthday" in 1867, is observed on July 1 with a national holiday. As many as one hundred thousand people will gather on Parliament Hill to listen to speeches and concerts, eat cake, and sing "O Canada." Everyone else goes to the cottage.

A spectacular sunset closes Canada Day.

DENIS DREVER / NCC / CCN

K

Kitchens

Apart from the food served in the Parliamentary DINING ROOM, which has its own kitchen and staff of cooks, all food on Parliament Hill is prepared in a central commissary kitchen in the West Block and delivered to cafeterias in all the buildings on the Hill. For a fee, the kitchen provides room service to MPs and senators in their offices. The two kitchens produce an average of forty thousand meals and snacks a month, using 3,400 litres of milk, 460 kilos of butter, and 1,200 kilos of FRENCH FRIES. *See also*: RESTAURANTS.

L

Landscaping

Parliament Hill was once a public gathering place where the citizens of Bytown, as Ottawa was originally called, met for picnics, bonfires, theatricals, and concerts. Officers of the British garrison pastured their cows on the Hill, and the soldiers planted potatoes to help feed themselves during the long winters. The grounds of the Hill have retained the open, informal style of the

Beds of colourful flowering annuals help make Parliament Hill one of Canada's most photogenic tourist attractions.

PAUL VON BAICH

public common and large numbers of people still gather here on July 1 or for DEMONSTRATIONS. Members of Parliament and their staff played baseball on the lawn until a tourist was knocked on the head by a fly ball, and a hundred years ago MPs and senators bowled on the lawn by the library. A summer house once perched on the bluff overlooking the river, a pleasant place for visitors to sit on a hot summer day. But from 1860 until 1866, and again from 1916 until 1920, the Hill was a dusty, windswept construction site crowded with workmen, scaffolding, and piles of stone (*see*: BUILDINGS). In recent years asphalt driveways and rows of parked cars have destroyed the original pastoral quality of the Hill, and there is constant agitation to relocate the parking lots. Ottawa's long, harsh winters and hot summers limit the kinds of trees and flowers that can be planted on the Hill.

Stands of pine keep it green in winter and complement the Gothic architecture. Thousands of tulip bulbs, originally a gift from the Dutch government, are set out in the fall to burst into bloom in late April. The tulips are replaced in May by colourful annuals that remain until the first frost in the fall. The lawns are kept free of litter and constantly sprinkled, mowed, and patched by a small army of gardeners and maintenance people employed by the National Capital Commission. In the winter, snow is removed from the Hill almost as soon as it falls. *See also*: STATUES.

Late Show

Opposition MPs are rarely satisfied with the replies they receive in QUESTION PERIOD, and every Monday, Tuesday, and Thursday from 5:30 p.m. to 6:00 p.m. five MPs can each make a four-minute speech to voice their dissatisfaction; the minister questioned has two minutes to reply. However ministers are not obliged to respond and may ignore both the question and the "late show" if they choose.

Lavatories

Public lavatories are located to the north of the West Block beneath the statue of Queen Victoria, who gave royal approval to the flush toilet by installing one in Buckingham Palace. The marble lavatories inside the Centre Block are off-limits to the public since 1966, when a man blew himself up in one with a homemade BOMB. *See also*: SECURITY.

Laws

See: ACT, BILL.

Leaders

Party leaders are elected by a majority of the delegates to a leadership convention. Delegates must be party members, and most are chosen by their constituency associations, although senators, MPs, and party executives have a large role to play in choosing the candidates. Parties have different rules for holding leadership conventions. A leader's performance may be reviewed regularly, and if his party's support is weak he is expected to resign. A party leader who loses one or two elections usually resigns. A leader does not have to be a member of Parliament when elected, but he is expected to seek a seat quickly, and an MP of the same party may vacate his seat to allow the leader to run. The goal of the party leader is to become prime minister, and rivalry for the leadership is fierce. Campaigns for delegates' votes last for months and are expensive for the contenders; however, losers who run a strong campaign are promoted in the party hierarchy, if only from fear, and MPs and delegates who support the winner receive recognition and preference. Broadcast on television from coast to coast, leadership conventions attract millions of viewers, who cheer for their favourites even though they may never vote for the party or the candidate. *See also*: PARTY.

Liberal Party

The Liberal Party is one of Canada's largest and oldest parties. Originally a coalition of reform parties, it grew out of popular demand for responsible government in the nineteenth century. Liberals advocated freedom of speech and religion, equality of opportunity, and economic development. Liberals supported Confederation in 1867 and the party elected its first federal government in 1874. Under Prime Minister Sir Wilfrid Laurier (1896-1911), the Liberals stood for western expansion, immigration, free trade with the United States, and equality for the French-Canadian population of Quebec. During the long premiership of W. L. Mackenzie King (1921-30, 1935-48), the Liberal Party became identified with social reform, national unity, independence from Great Britain, and economic pragmatism. Liberal Prime Minister Lester B. Pearson (1963-68) established Canada's reputation as an international peacekeeper. Prime Minister Pierre Elliott Trudeau (1968-79, 1980-84) instituted a policy of national bilingualism, encouraged state ownership of energy resources, and gave Canada the Constitution of 1982 and Charter of Rights and Freedoms. *See also*: PROGRESSIVE CONSERVATIVE PARTY, NEW DEMOCRACTIC PARTY.

The Library miraculously escaped the fire that destroyed the adjoining Centre Block in February 1916. Construction began on a new Centre Block as soon as the walls of the old building were cleared away.

Library of Parliament

Designed by the architects of the original Centre Block, Thomas Fuller and Chilion Jones, the Parliamentary Library is a superb example of ornate Gothic Revival and a building of beauty, serenity, and charm. It appears to be round, but it has sixteen walls supported by massive flying buttresses. The Library is 132 feet high and 90 feet wide, and the interior is dominated by a soaring cupola that dwarfs the reference room beneath. Natural light from the windows around the base of the cupola highlights the white marble statue of Queen Victoria in the centre of the room and gives the library a subdued brightness conducive to contemplation. The three tiers of shelves are arranged in bays with a reading table in each one; the floors of the tiers, now wooden, were originally made of glass. The shelves and desks are made of Ontario white pine hand carved in hundreds of different Gothic patterns (*see:* WOOD CARVING).The parquet floor is cherry, oak, and walnut. The wood adds warmth and colour to the library and absorbs the sound.

Opened in 1876 with a ball given by the members of Parliament, the library narrowly escaped the FIRE of 1916, and it was nearly destroyed in 1952 when a small fire started in the roof: water and smoke damaged nearly one-third of the library's collection and turned the reading room into a lake. Restoration took four years, but most of the books and furniture were saved.

The original building is only the visible part of the Library's current operation. With more than six hundred thousand books in its collection, as well as microfilm, newspapers, and periodicals, the library has branches in several buildings on Parliament Hill and it is linked to individual offices by computer. As well as lending books and periodicals, more than

In the Library, an enormous vaulted dome soars over tiers of carved shelves and a white marble statue of young Queen Victoria.

CANAPRESS

With its diffuse light and golden pine panelling the Library radiates medieval tranquility, but it provides sophisticated computerized service for MPs, senators, and members of the press gallery.

PAUL VON BAICH

two hundred and fifty staff members answer questions, prepare bibliographies, draft background papers, and assist committees; the Library also provides a specialized RESEARCH service. Until 1953 the Parliamentary Library was also the National Library; it now serves only MPs, senators, and their staff, and the Press Gallery.

Liquor

Canada's first prime minister, Sir John A. Macdonald, was notorious for his drinking bouts, which didn't seem to impede his political judgement or his popularity. Early political meetings were often held in front of saloons to guarantee the politicians an audience, and on election day jugs of whisky were passed around to woo votes or to make opponents incapable of voting at all. In frontier Canada, where thousands of people were isolated on homesteads in the bush, an election campaign was an excuse to get together and whoop it up, and liquor was an accepted part of the political process until government regulations restricted the sale and consumption of liquor in public places and banned it on election day.

Members of Parliament have traditionally relied on "spirits" to increase their eloquence, sometimes to the point of incoherence, and to establish the convivial bonds of friendship essential to a successful parliamentary career. The original Centre Block had a saloon located directly beneath the Commons chamber, with steps leading down behind the Speaker's chair, and during debate a steady procession of honourable members wound up and down the staircase to the saloon. As debate progressed, many MPs became so drunk and rowdy the business of the House was virtually brought to a standstill. The saloon was eliminated from the House of Commons when the Centre Block was rebuilt, but the saloons in nearby hotels were equally popular. Many MPs also kept a stock of liquor in their filing cabinets. Bootlegging has always been part of life on Parliament Hill, and staff members are occasionally apprehended smuggling in cheap, contraband liquor, but the arrival of television cameras in the chamber in 1977 had a sobering effect on debate. Only the Parliamentary dining room has a liquor licence, but bottles of gin and whisky may be purchased from a small liquor store in the basement of the Centre Block.

Lobby

Behind the curtains along both sides of the Commons chamber, MPs can relax in a narrow, carpeted lobby when they want to take a break. Screened from the galleries and the Speaker, the lobbies permit MPs to put their feet up, read, or talk together while keeping an ear on the debate. During a heated debate or a political crisis, MPs gather in their lobbies to discuss party strategy, and they assemble there in anticipation of a VOTE.

Lobbyists

Everybody with an axe to grind with the government wants the support of MPs in order to promote or defeat a particular piece of legislation, win a contract, or advocate a policy. Petitioners traditionally accosted MPs as they came and went from the lobbies, but lobbyists now behave much more discreetly. Influential MPs are pestered, entertained, and sent on exotic trips by lobbyists representing corporations, foreign countries, charities, trade unions, and arts organizations. Lobbying is a legitimate and acceptable activity, but MPs who appear to be "bought" by a particular interest group can get into political trouble. Since 1988 lobbyists have been required to register, and about three thousand have done so. *See also*: CORRUPTION, MEDIA, SCANDAL.

Lover's Walk.

NATIONAL ARCHIVES OF CANADA / C-1542

Lovers' Walk

When Parliament Hill was still a British garrison, water was hauled up the bluff from the Ottawa River, and the path the water wagons made through the trees later became a popular retreat for politicians seeking a breath of fresh air or a place to hold a confidential conversation. Benches were installed facing the river, and in the evenings the path became a rendezvous for young lovers. During the Depression, Prime Minister R. B. Bennett became fearful that the bluff would become a campground for vagrants and radicals and the walk was closed.

M

Mace

In the Middle Ages the sergeants-at-arms of the royal bodyguard carried heavy round-headed wooden clubs spiked with iron to ward off attacks on the king. A deadly weapon capable of piercing armour, the mace became the symbol of the king's power, and now symbolizes the authority of the Crown vested in Parliament. The mace is carried by the Sergeant-at-Arms, who preceeds the Speaker into the Commons chamber with the mace resting on his right shoulder. When the House is in session, the mace rests in brackets on the TABLE of the House; when the House sits as a committee and the Speaker is not in the chair, the mace rests beneath the table. The mace still symbolizes the Sergeant-at-Arms' authority to arrest or disperse troublemakers, but it no longer resembles a weapon of war. Canada's present mace, a gift from the silversmiths of London, England, after the original mace was destroyed in the fire of 1916, is gilded sterling silver engraved with Canada's coat of arms, the English rose, the Scottish thistle, the Irish shamrock, the French fleur-de-lis, and the initials "E. R." for the queen, Elizabeth Regina. It contains the melted remnant of the original mace. When not in use, the mace is kept in a locked glass cupboard in the Speaker's office. *See also*: SERGEANT-AT-ARMS, SPEAKER.

Maple Leaf

The maple leaf has supplanted the English rose, the Scottish thistle, the Irish shamrock, and the French fleur-de-lis as Canada's recognized symbol, although many people in the province of Quebec prefer the fleur-de-lis, and few maple trees grow west of Ontario. *See*: FLAG.

Media

See: PRESS GALLERY, TELEVISION.

Mediation Room

Inside the south entrance to the East Block a comfortable room has been set aside for contemplation and prayer in memory of a young Conservative MP, Sean O'Sullivan, who left politics for the priesthood and later died of cancer. The room has an altar handmade and carved by a member of the Commons' carpentry staff, and can be used for weddings, memorial services, and religious observances as well as meditation. "All of us need spiritual reflection, and those that think they don't are the ones that need it the most," said Speaker John Fraser when the room was dedicated in March 1991.

Members of Parliament

Any Canadian citizen age eighteen or over can become a member of Parliament if he has not served five years or more in jail. The trick is to get elected. Unless he runs as an Independent, a candidate must first be nominated by a political party's constituency branch, and nominations are often hotly contested, especially when the seat is considered safe. Many MPs work their way up through the party ranks; others achieve distinction in business or the professions before entering politics. The majority of MPs are middle-aged, middle-class, and male. They also tend to be wealthier and more conservative than the people they represent, but they try to express the changing views of the public. Since MPs require no particular training or qualifications for their job, they learn

A typical member of Parliament, John Harvard, at work in his office.

MONE CHENG PHOTOGRAPHY
STUDIO

about governing by doing it. Being an MP is a full-time job. Some work twelve hours a day, seven days a week; others treat their term as a paid vacation.

An MP has three main responsibilities: to represent and assist his constituents, whether they voted for him or not; to support his party; to contribute according to his conscience and talents, whether in government or opposition. Most of an MP's work is done out of the public eye, in CAUCUS and COMMITTEE, at breakfast, on the phone, or in his office, and an MP who works hard for his constituents is more assured of re-election than one who makes speeches in the House. An MP's work is often tedious, tiring, and unrewarding; some find the endless grind and the strain of separation from their families too great, others thrive on the rubber-chicken circuit. No amount of work or handshaking will guarantee victory: Canadians tend to vote by party and policy rather than personality. *See also*: CONSTITUENCY, HOUSE OF COMMONS, PARTY, PARTIES, SALARIES, WHIP.

Memorial Chamber

The PEACE TOWER was built to commemorate Canada's role in the First World War, and within the tower the sombre Memorial chamber now honours the memory of all Canadians who have served their country since it was a colony of France. The stone used in this beautiful small room was supplied by Canada's original allies in the First World War: the pale white walls are Château Gaillard stone from France, the altar is white limestone from England, and the altar steps are Belgian black marble. The floor is of stone quarried from areas where Canadians fought, inlaid with brass plaques made from shell casings and inscribed with the names of the major battles. On three sides of the chamber, stained-glass windows depict allegorical scenes: The Call to Arms, The Assembly of Remembrance, and The Dawn of Peace. The badges and insignia of Canadian regiments are carved into the stone walls, as are scenes depicting Canada's military history. Two stone figures of women, Recording Angel and War Widow, stand near the door. Four BOOKS OF REMEMBRANCE are placed around the sides of the chamber; the book commemorating the dead of the First World War is on the altar guarded by four kneeling, bronze angels. An inscription from Paul Bunyan's *Pilgrim's Progress* is inscribed around the altar: "My marks and scars I carry with me to be a witness for me that I have fought

Capturing the impressive height of the Memorial chamber, this photograph by Chris Lund gives the illusion that the walls are curved.

CHRIS LUND / NATIONAL ARCHIVES OF CANADA

his battles who now will be my rewarder. So he passed over and all the trumpets sounded." John McCrae's famous poem, "In Flanders Fields," is engraved on the east wall; two stone lions by the door carry shields bearing the dragon of war and the dove of peace. The Memorial Chamber is open to TOURISTS year round during regular hours. See TOURS.

Messengers

Before electricity came to Parliament Hill, politicians had to rely on people to deliver information and run errands, and both the House of Commons and Senate still employ uniformed messengers. Messengers can be entrusted to be quick and confidential and are permitted to leave the Hill in the course of their work; however, their business may not always be public or political. *See also*: LIQUOR, SCANDAL.

Ministers

See: CABINET.

Naming

When an MP swears, screams, shakes his fist, or insults another member in the House, he is asked by the Speaker to apologize. If he refuses or continues to be rude and disorderly, the Speaker can have the MP removed from the Commons chamber for the rest of the day's sitting. In being told to leave, the MP is addressed by his actual name rather than as "The Honourable Member," a gesture that symbolically deprives him of the rights and privileges of the House. MPs who are named usually leave voluntarily, but, if necessary, they can be bodily removed by the Sergeant-at-Arms and the security staff. They usually aplogize and return at the next day's sitting. *See also*: DECORUM.

New Democratic Party

Traditionally the third largest political party in the House of Commons, the NDP usually wins between 25 and 45 of the 295 seats. Philosophically to the left of the Liberal Party, the NDP advocates programs of social welfare, medicare, equality of opportunity, and disarmament. It was formed in 1961 as a result of the merger of its predecessor, the Co-operative Commonwealth Federation, with the leading labour unions, and its origins go back to two Labour members of Parliament, J. S. Woodsworth and A. A. Heaps, who were elected to the House of Commons in 1921. The Co-operative Commonwealth Federation advocated socialist programs of state ownership, but the present NDP favours a partnership between government, labour, and business. The NDP has never formed a federal government, but it has at various times achieved power in the provinces of Saskatchewan, Manitoba, British Columbia, Ontario, and the Yukon Territory. *See also*: LIBERAL PARTY, PROGRESSIVE CONSERVATIVE PARTY, WOMEN.

No Comment

The standard response of MPs, particularly prime ministers, who are caught in embarrassing situations. *See also*: SCRUM

Nurses

With a population of four thousand, a million tourists, and countless visitors each year, Parliament Hill suffers a number of daily casualties. Headaches, indigestion, and minor injuries are treated by a staff of nurses at four health units on the Hill; the nurses also provide counselling for people suffering from stress and anxiety caused by political or personal problems. The nursing stations receive about twelve thousand visits a year. MPs and senators also have access to an Ottawa military hospital.

O

Oasis

In 1984, Parliament Hill was linked together by a closed-circuit central cable system called Office Automation Services and Information Systems. OASIS enables staff and members of Parliament to communicate with each other by electronic mail: letters or messages typed on a computer keyboard are transmitted to computer screens elsewhere on the Hill. MPs are also able to send electronic messages to their constituencies thousands of miles away; complaints and grievances from the public can be dealt with more quickly than by mail and more accurately than by telephone. While OASIS can use outside telephone lines and data banks, OASIS cannot be entered by outside users. To protect the security and confidentiality of political communications, every MP is given a private number and password; if someone tries to read his electronic mail, OASIS will warn him that his code is not secure. OASIS has helped reduce the size of the staff on the Hill, but the amount of paper used has actually increased. *See also*: TELEVISION.

Oath of Allegiance

Every MP must be sworn into office before he is allowed to take his seat in the Commons chamber. The ceremony usually takes place in the Clerk's office a few days before the OPENING of Parliament. The MP is allowed to invite his family, friends, and a photographer, but if a large number of MPs are waiting to be sworn in the ceremony can be very rushed: before one session the clerks were swearing in MPs lined up in the hall. After taking the oath, the member signs his name in the roll of the House. The oath is very simple: "I do swear that I will be faithful and bear true allegiance to Her Majesty Queen Elizabeth II." Since it does not contain the word "Canada," the oath is sometimes misunderstood as allegiance to Great Britain. *See also*: CROWN, QUEEN.

O Canada

Canada's national anthem is not the most lyrical or imaginative in the world, but it makes up in simplicity what it lacks in genius. Sung on public occasions in French since 1880 and in English since 1908, "O Canada" was officially adopted as the national anthem in 1980 after two other popular anthems, "God Save the Queen" and "The Maple Leaf Forever," fell out of favour. "God Save the Queen" is too British and "The Maple Leaf Forever" has the same tune as "America the Beautiful." The French lyrics to "O Canada" are completely different. The English version of the first verse is:

"O Canada, our home and native land,
True patriot love in all thy sons command.
With glowing hearts we see thee rise,
The True North strong and free.
From far and wide, O Canada,
We stand on guard for thee.
God keep our land glorious and free,
O Canada, we stand on guard for thee,
O Canada, we stand on guard for thee."

Offices

An MP's office is his castle and he may do there more or less as he pleases, except smoke. He may shout and weep, drink, sleep, eat, fight, make love, watch television, talk on the phone, or attempt to avoid arrest: the police are not allowed to search an MP's office without the permission of the Speaker. In 1945 police feared that an MP wanted for espionage, Fred Rose, might hole up in the House, but Rose was arrested at his home. Before night sittings were abolished in 1982, some MPs virtually lived in their offices: they had hideaway beds, electric

The most beautiful office on the Hill: the original West Block office of Prime Minister Alexander Mackenzie (1873-78). Note the height of the ceiling, the thickness of the stone walls, and the antique washroom in its own turret. The room also has a secret passageway.

MONE CHENG PHOTOGRAPHY STUDIO

Canada's first prime minister, Sir John A. Macdonald, worked in this East Block office, which has been restored to look as it did in the 1880s when Macdonald was at the height of his power.

PAUL VON BAICH

kettles, hot plates, toaster ovens, refrigerators, dishes, cutlery, sinks, towels, and a change of clothes in the closet. One MP had twin beds: he was told that the House was not a rooming house. Now MPs usually leave by 7:00 p.m., and fire regulations restrict the kitchen to a coffee maker.

Offices vary in size from dark cubbyholes under the eaves to palatial suites with thick carpet and high ceilings. Offices are allocated by the party WHIPS in consultation with the Commons staff, and ambitious MPs connive shamelessly to get the best. Although many of the offices in the Centre Block are cramped and antiquated, it remains the most prestigious location. New MPs are banished to the Confederation Building or the Wellington Building across the street. *See also*: CLEANERS, FURNITURE, INTERIOR DECORATING, SCANDAL, SENATE.

Oh! Oh!

Debates in the House are recorded verbatim and published the next day in HANSARD. Rather than attempting to transcribe the cacophany of catcalls, insults, hoots, and yells with which MPs often respond to their opponents' arguments, Hansard reporters substitute the standard phrase, "Some hon. members: Oh! Oh!" The honourable members are definitely not saying "Oh! Oh!" but what they are saying is unprintable. *See also*: UNPARLIAMENTARY.

Opening

The opening of a new session of Parliament is conducted with impressive pomp and ceremony, especially when it is a new Parliament following a general election. Senators, scarlet-robed judges of the Supreme Court, the diplomatic corps, and official guests gather in the Senate chamber to await the arrival of the governor general to read the Speech from the Throne. The governor general drives to Parliament Hill in a limousine or an open carriage, accompanied by his aides-de-camp and officers of the armed forces. At the main entrance to the Centre Block the governor general receives a twenty-one gun royal salute, then walks to the Senate chamber accompanied by the prime minister, the government leader of the Senate, and a military escort. When they have taken their

The Opening of a session of Parliament in the Senate chamber. Guests line both sides of the chamber and the judges of the Supreme Court face the Governor General, who reads the Throne Speech from his chair beneath the canopy.

CANAPRESS

places, BLACK ROD is dispatched to the Commons chamber where the MPs have gathered to await the royal summons. Finding the oak doors of the Commons chamber closed, Black Rod knocks three times with his stick to summon the MPs to the Senate chamber. Led by the Speaker, the MPs make their way down the hall in a crowd, walking slowly to assert their independence from the orders of the Queen's representative. They gather at the BAR just inside the door to the Senate chamber, latecomers and backbenchers spilling out into the ante-room and the Senate foyer. Seated on the throne, the governor general reads the Speech from the Throne in both English and French. The Throne Speech, outlining government policy, is written by the prime minister and gives a brief survey of the policies the government intends to pursue during the session. Following the ceremony an informal reception is held in the HALL OF HONOUR.

The Opening of a session was once much more elaborate. Men wore black tie, military uniform, or court uniform with medals, and their wives were decked out in low-cut ballgowns and all the jewellery they could beg, borrow, or buy. Parading through the dusty streets of Ottawa half-naked at 10:00 a.m. struck many women as ridiculous, and the formality was gradually relaxed. Men and women now wear business suits or elegant street clothes, no one bows or curtsys to the governor general, and the custom of presenting debutants to the governor general after the Opening has disappeared. However when Queen Elizabeth II opened Parliament in 1957 and 1977, the ceremony was conducted with more traditional royal fanfare. *See also*: GOVERNOR GENERAL, SENATE, SESSION.

Opposition

The party that wins the second largest number of seats in the House of Commons forms Her Majesty's Loyal Opposition. Opposition MPs sit on the Speaker's left, the government on his right. The role of the Opposition is to criticize government legislation, attack cabinet ministers in debate, scrutinize their personal and political conduct, condemn the way they are running the country, and nurse ambitions of becoming the government themselves. Since 1921 Canada has had a multi-party system with several parties in opposition, but only the Conservatives or the Liberals have ever formed the Official Opposition. Leaders of opposition parties receive larger offices, higher salaries, and more PERKS than their colleagues, but for backbenchers a career in opposition can mean years of hard work and obscurity. *See also*: GOVERNMENT.

Order!

When debate comes too noisy and boisterous, the SPEAKER may repeatedly call out "Order! Order!" until the MPs have settled down. If this doesn't work, the Speaker stands. This forces all MPs in the House to sit down and effectively brings debate to a halt. The Speaker can also push a button on the arm of his chair that turns off all MPs' desk microphones and renders them virtually inaudible. The Speaker's reputation rests on his or her ability to maintain order in the House, although visitors are often shocked at the level of noise and the vulgarity of some members' conduct, especially during QUESTION PERIOD. *See also*: DECORUM, NAMING.

Orders of the Day

The business of Parliament is conducted according to a timetable distributed to all MPs every morning. The Order Paper gives notice of motions that may be presented later, and an appended "Projected Orders" lists the motions coming up for debate that day. Some motions that have not been listed on the Order Paper can be made on the floor of the House, including a motion calling for the House to adjourn or to debate a national emergency. *See also*: CLERK, DEBATE.

Other Place

Although MPs and senators are often close personal friends and political colleagues, the House of Commons and the Senate are jealous of their separate powers. Rather than refer to the other chamber by name, or even acknowledge its existence, they refer to it as "the other place" or "another place." This quaint custom causes some befuddlement among newcomers to the Hill: one senator thought the "other place" meant Heaven.

Ottawa

Accurately described as "a sub-Arctic lumber village," Ottawa was chosen as Canada's capital by Queen Victoria in 1858. It was a controversial decision. Ottawa was a ragged settlement of lumber mills, saloons, and military barracks hundreds of miles from nowhere, but this was precisely what attracted the Queen: Ottawa was far enough from the American border to be safe from invasion, yet it was connected to Toronto, Kingston, and Montreal by the Rideau Canal. Situated on the border between Ontario and Quebec, Ottawa was both French and English, and its location provided a spectacular site for the Parliament Buildings.

Ottawa is still a small isolated city, but it has history, beauty, and charm, and like Washington, D.C., its personality and architecture are shaped by its political function. The wilderness still stretches away to the northwest, and while the lumber mills have disappeared, Ottawa still runs on paper. On weekdays it rolls up the sidewalks at 6:00 p.m. *See also*: TOURISTS.

P

Pages

Both the Senate and the House of Commons employ first-year university students to act as pages in their respective chambers while Parliament is in session. Dressed in black uniforms and white shirts, the pages sit on the steps of the dias below the Speaker's chair and jump up whenever someone beckons or when the Speaker stands. Bright, bilingual, and politically non-partisan, the pages fetch and carry glasses of water, documents, and notes, enabling the MPs and senators to remain in touch with their offices and to communicate with each other without leaving the chamber. In the nineteenth-century, pages were hired as young as age eleven and required to quit at seventeen; they could not be more than five foot six inches tall – in case they obscured the view in the chamber –

Pages no longer have to be short, or male, but they use their feet.

MONE CHENG PHOTOGRAPHY STUDIO

and all were boys. Now pages of both sexes are recruited from across Canada on the basis of academic excellence. They must also be well-mannered and well-groomed. The House of Commons has forty-two pages; between ten and fourteen are on duty at various times during a sitting, and each page works about fifteen hours a week.

Parliament

Derived from the French word *parler*, to talk, Parliament is a public forum where laws are made through a process of discussion and resolution. Parliament originated in the Middle Ages when the English king summoned representatives of the lords, the church, and the commoners to Westminster to help him raise taxes and maintain law and order. Over the centuries, the power of the commoners, or Commons, surpassed that of the king, largely because the people refused to pay their taxes unless he did as he was told. In the seventeenth-century, King Charles I of England claimed to have a divine right to rule without Parliament. He charged several MPs with treason and attacked the House of Commons with armed troops. The people rose in revolt; King Charles's troops were defeated by commoners led by Oliver Cromwell, and the King was executed; the monarchy was restored, but in 1688 James II was dethroned. Since then the supremacy of Parliament has not been seriously challenged by the monarch.

According to Beauchesne's *Parliamentary Rules and Forms*, the principles of Canadian parliamentary law are: to protect a minority and restrain the improvidence or tyranny of a majority; to secure the transaction of public business in an orderly manner; to enable every member to express opinions within limits necessary to preserve decorum and prevent an unnecessary waste of time; to give abundant opportunity for the consideration of every measure, and to prevent any legislative action being taken upon impulse. *See also*: HOUSE OF COMMONS, QUEEN.

Parties

Members of Parliament are sociable, talkative, energetic, and lonely. Away from their homes and families for days and weeks at a time, they spend most of their time together and form strong friendships that cross party lines. Parliament Hill is often compared to an expensive club, and schmoozing can be as important as political debate. Social activities enable MPs to meet each other in a relaxed and friendly atmosphere away from the public eye and the tensions of the Commons chamber, and they foster the informal relationships that make the business of governing run smoothly. Parliament Hill is in a constant tizzy of birthday celebrations, banquets, pancake breakfasts, lobster feasts, champagne receptions, and office cocktails (*see*: WEDNESDAY). MPs are also expected to entertain their constituents, party workers, and staff, and some do it so well they are re-elected for years. The MPs receive a substantial expense allowance, but it is never enough. *See also*: SALARIES, SENATE.

Party

Almost as soon as men and women began meeting together to resolve their problems in a democratic way, they divided into factions based on personal and ideological differences. Democracy recognizes the right of the majority to rule, as long as it respects the rights of minorities, and the political party system has grown out of this perpetual contest for power. Canada has numerous political parties, some very small, which are born, grow, diminish, and sometimes disappear according to the preferences of the people. Party membership is cheap and available to every citizen; most parties have youth branches for those under voting age. Belonging to a party allows ordinary citizens to become involved in politics without running for office: party members raise money, distribute literature, choose delegates to elect the leader, campaign in elections, and help determine party policy. An MP spends a great deal of time with his party supporters (*see*: CONSTITUENCY). He does not have to take their advice or follow their orders – he must represent *all* his constituents – but an MP who antagonizes his party workers or fails to follow party policy may soon be out of a job. In the past, representatives of the minority Créditiste, Communist, Labour, Progressive, and the Social Credit parties have sat in the House of Commons; they have been followed by the Bloc Québécois and the Reform Party. Canada has dozens of small political parties, including the Green Party and the satirical Rhinoceros party.

Political parties try to be tightly organized and highly disciplined; an MP is expected to be loyal to his party through thick and thin and to vote in the Commons according to party policy, although he may disagree with the policy on a particular bill. Critics complain that party loyalty turns MPs into trained seals, and MPs who disobey party orders are labelled "mavericks" or "renegades." In fact parties are often disorganized, particularly during leadership campaigns, and an independent-minded candidate who is in touch with popular thinking will sometimes beat out those who toe the party line. *See also*: LEADER, MEMBER OF PARLIAMENT, WHIP.

Patronage

The prime minister has the responsibility for appointing senators, federal court judges, ambassadors, and members of federal boards, commissions, councils, and corporations. Apart from judges, who take no part in politics, these positions too frequently go to the prime minister's personal friends and party supporters as a reward for loyalty and service. Patronage appointments do not reward merit or encourage efficiency, and since some of the positions carry high salaries, those who get these plums are fiercely criticized by those who don't. Patronage also takes the form of government contracts awarded to businessmen who contribute financially to the government party, and contracts for public buildings constructed in the ridings of powerful cabinet ministers and MPs: the minister of Public Works is usually an influential member of the cabinet. Opposition parties constantly promise to reform or abolish patronage, but government parties always find much to recommend it.

Peace Tower

Originally informally called the Victory or Victoria Tower, the 300-foot Peace Tower was added to the new Centre Block to commemorate Canada's sacrifice in the First World War, 1914-18, and it provides a dramatic entrance to the Parliament buildings. The south arch of the tower is flanked by the lion and the unicorn and surmounted by an inscription from Psalm 72: "Give the King thy judgements O God, and thy righteousness unto the King's son." The east arch bears another inscription from Psalm 72: "He shall have dominion from sea unto sea," and the west arch a line from Proverbs: "Where there is no vision the peo-

The Peace Tower in 1923. Construction of the tower was halted for more than a year because of the cost, a not uncommon complaint on Parliament Hill.

NATIONAL ARCHIVES OF CANADA / PA-31010

ple perish." Over the main door-
way is inscribed: "The wholesome
sea is at her gates, her gates both
east and west." The Peace Tower
contains the MEMORIAL CHAMBER,
which is entered from the third
floor, and above it the fifty-three
bells of the CARILLON and the carillonneur's room. An elevator takes
visitors to the Memorial chamber
and to a glassed-in observation
deck below the clock face which
offers a superb view of the Ottawa
River and the Gatineau Hills. The
Peace Tower was officially dedicated on July 1, 1927, Canada's
Diamond Jubilee.

In July 1921, the Peace Tower begins to rise over
Parliament Hill.

NATIONAL ARCHIVES OF CANADA / C-38750

Perks

Because Parliament was originally summoned by the king under his protection, its members traditionally enjoy some privileges, or perks, denied to
other citizens. Members of Parliament receive free paper, printing, and postage
within their budget, and anyone may write to an MP at the House of Commons
free of charge. An MP's telephone is free and he is supplied with at least two
computers, a printer, two television sets, and a fax machine. MPs also are given
free railway travel anywhere in Canada and an airline pass to enable them to
commute back and forth to their constituencies: the pass extends to members of
the MP's family, but the number of trips is limited to approximately sixty-four a
year. Meals in the Parliamentary dining room cost less than an equivalent restau-
rant downtown, and the food in the House of Commons' cafeterias is very
cheap. The Speaker, senior cabinet ministers, the prime minister, and the leaders

of the major opposition parties are entitled to limousines, some with relays of drivers, and the prime minister, whose licence plate is CAN 001, travels in a bullet-proof Cadillac with a police escort. The prime minister and members of the cabinet also have the use of government aircraft, and both the PM and the leader of the Opposition are provided with free residences in Ottawa (*see:* 24 SUSSEX DRIVE, STORNOWAY). MPs also have the opportunity to travel at public expense to conventions and conferences around the world, although if they take too many free trips to unpopular countries, or misbehave when there, they could be in political trouble. *See also*: LOBBYISTS, SALARIES, SCANDAL.

Petitions

Citizens who want Parliament to redress a grievance or address a particular problem may ask an MP to present their petition to the House of Commons. A petition must be signed by at least twenty-five people, state the problem in clear, respectful language, and request specific action. Petitions cannot deal with matters beyond the jurisdiction of the House of Commons or within the jurisdiction of the courts; they should also not require the spending of public money. MPs may present the petition verbally in the House or submit it to the Clerk; all petitions receive a reply and may result in legislation. Between five thousand and nine thousand petitions are presented to the House of Commons during every session.

PMO

Popularly known as the "dreaded PMO," the Prime Minister's Office is the political hub around which the government revolves. In 1867, the PRIME MINISTER had one secretary; in 1873 he answered all his mail himself. Now he has a principal secretary and a staff of more than one hundred. The PMO occupies the Langevin block across from Parliament Hill, although the prime minister's private office is on the third floor of the Centre Block next to the Cabinet room. The function of the PMO is to protect and promote the personal interests of the prime minister – to get him re-elected – and the PMO is staffed by political cronies and flacks, image-makers, consultants, and spin-doctors, who operate as the PM's eyes

The office of the prime minister's secretary in the 1880s.

NATIONAL ARCHIVES OF CANADA / PA-9001

and ears on the Hill and across the country. They write his speeches, organize his schedule, boost his ego, and shield him from enemies and pratfalls. The present PMO also includes an office for the prime minister's wife. The PMO is so secretive and powerful it has been described as the Canadian White House, and its power is resented by cabinet ministers and party members who feel excluded. The cost of the PMO is paid by the taxpayers, but the exact amount and details of its budget are almost impossible to discover. When the prime minister is defeated, his staff resigns with him. *See also*: PRIME MINISTER, PRIVY COUNCIL OFFICE.

Poker

The House of Commons was once the site of a floating poker game that ran day and night during sessions of Parliament, its location and players changing according to the demands of sleep and politics. Stakes were high, fortunes were won and lost, and political careers were risked on a turn of the cards. The abolition of night sittings of the House of Commons in 1982 put a damper on the backstage nightlife of Parliament Hill, and although there are still a few dedicated players, poker has gone the way of the spitoon and saloon. *See also*: SCANDAL.

Portraits

There are approximately 125 portraits of kings, queens, prime ministers, and Speakers in the Parliament buildings. The portraits of prime ministers Lester B. Pearson, John G. Diefenbaker, and Pierre E. Trudeau hang in the corridor joining the ROTUNDA to the House of Commons FOYER; portraits of earlier prime ministers, including Sir John A. Macdonald, hang on the walls of the foyer. Two nineteenth-century prime ministers, Sir Mackenzie Bowell and Sir John Abbott are missing, and three prime ministers since 1979 have not yet had their portraits painted. Portraits of past Speakers line the Speaker's corridor. The British kings and queens – Queen Victoria, King George III and Queen Charlotte, King Edward VII and Queen Alexandra

This famous portrait of young Queen Victoria now hangs in the foyer of the Senate chamber.

NATIONAL ARCHIVES OF CANADA / PC-111206 / COURTESY OF THE SENATE OF CANADA

– are in the Senate foyer. The portraits vary greatly in quality and style and are not necessarily accurate: Prime Minister Diefenbaker's eyes were blue, not brown as depicted, and Queen Victoria did not have a shrunken left arm as her portrait by John Partridge suggests. Queen Victoria was held in such high regard in Canada that when fire swept through the Centre Block in 1916 her portrait was one of the few things rescued; it had been saved from the flames three times before, once in 1849 when the Assembly House in Montreal was set on fire, and twice more when the hotels where it was stored burned to the ground. *See also:* FIRE, HISTORY.

Post Office

The House of Commons and the Senate have separate, adjoining post offices in the basement of the Centre Block. Each MP and senator has a private box with a key and it is well used: an estimated 60 million pieces of mail a year pass through the Commons' post office alone. MPs get mail pick-up and delivery every twenty minutes while the House is in session, senators on the hour. The delivery service circulates inter-office mail and distributes reports, bills, JOURNALS, and HANSARD. *See also*: MESSENGERS, OASIS.

Prayer

At the start of each day's sitting, before the doors to the Commons chamber are opened to admit the public, the Speaker reads a long, traditional prayer in both English and French beseeching God to "direct and prosper" the Queen, the Royal Family, Canada, the governor general, the Senate, and the House of Commons "that all things may be so ordered and settled by their endeavours upon the best and surest foundations that peace and happiness, truth and justice, religion and piety may be established among us for all generations." The prayer concludes with a short version of the Lord's Prayer, which ends appropriately, "And lead us not into temptation, but deliver us from evil." Its British emphasis and Church of England tone make the prayer unpopular with many MPs who do not enter the chamber until later. *See also*: SITTING.

Precinct

As the number of MPs increased and the size of government operations grew far beyond the scale imagined in 1867, the precinct of Parliament Hill gradually expanded to include the Confederation, Langevin, Victoria, and Wellington buildings on Wellington Street and La Promenade building on Sparks Street, as well as rented office space several blocks away. The East, West, and Centre blocks are linked by TUNNELS, and all buildings by BUSES and the OASIS electronic computer system. The offices and activities of the House of Commons come under the jurisdiction of the Speaker; the Senate precinct is run by the Senate's Standing Committee on Internal Economy.

Press Gallery

T he freedom of the press to publish reports of Parliamentary debates and to comment on the behaviour of political leaders was won only after hundreds of years of bitter and violent struggle in Great Britain. Until the eighteenth century, parliamentary debates took place in virtual secrecy, partly because MPs feared they might be arrested for treason if the king learned about critical remarks made about him in the protected confines of the Commons chamber (*see*: PRIVILEGE). In a society racked by religious and civil war, men often paid with their lives for their opinions, and printers or journalists who published reports of House of Commons debates were imprisoned or outlawed. However, the public demanded to be told what their elected leaders were up to, and the growing popularity of newspaper journalism made secrecy impossible to maintain. Joining the Lords, the Church, and the Commons, the press became the

The press gallery about one hundred years ago when reporters took down speeches in shorthand and telegraphed their stories to their newspapers. The sink, water cooler, and spitoon were fixtures on the Hill for generations.

NATIONAL ARCHIVES OF CANADA / PA-48151

The press gallery in 1991.

MONE CHENG PHOTOGRAPHY STUDIO

"fourth estate" of a constitutional monarchy and entitled to share in the privileges of Parliament as the eyes, ears, and conscience of the people.

In Canada, the power of the media has increased to the point where critics complain it exceeds the influence of the MPs themselves. Because journalists are not allowed to take cameras and tape recorders into the Commons chamber, politicians often choose to make policy announcements or critical comments outside the House for the benefit of television and radio reporters, thereby speaking directly to the people rather than to their colleagues in the House. The role of the fourth estate is to publicize everything that goes on in the process of government, and the media are more effective than the Opposition in revealing CORRUPTION and SCANDAL.

The Parliamentary Press Gallery has 365 full-time members and 2,000 temporary or part-time members, including television and radio producers and technicians. An annual fee of fifty dollars entitles a full member to a parking spot, access to the Parliamentary dining room, the services of the Library, and wide freedom to roam the Parliamentary precinct.

The long, narrow gallery above the Speaker's chair in the House of Commons is only the visible part of the Press Gallery, and few reporters sit in the chamber unless there is a crisis or a vote. Gone are the days when reporters took down debates in shorthand and telegraphed their stories to their newspapers; now they watch on television and send their stories by computer or wait to grab an MP in a SCRUM. Gallery reporters were originally accommodated in a large newsroom on the third floor of the Centre Block, but as their numbers increased their desks and typewriters spilled out into the corridor and the entire northeast hallway became the press gallery. Reeking of whisky, cigars, and gossip, the gallery was a den of iniquity where MPs, aides, and senators went to trade stories, circulate rumours, drink, and tell jokes. In 1960, the hallway was cleared, and most of the reporters moved across the street to the National Press Building at 150 Wellington Street, leaving only freelancers and small bureaus in the original gallery. The National Press Building also houses a small theatre for press conferences and the private bar and dining room of the Press Club; the annual Press Gallery dinner is held in the Parliamentary dining room, followed by an evening of raucous jokes and satirical skits. Politics is news in Canada. Television reporters and newspaper columnists become celebrities, and the daily political drama is followed as avidly as a soap opera or hockey game. *See also*: TELEVISION.

Prime Minister

The role of prime minister emerged in the eighteenth century when the German-born king of England, George I, stayed away from meetings of his cabinet because he didn't understand a word of English. With the king absent, the most influential cabinet minister took charge of proceedings, and although his power was deeply resented by his colleagues, the "first minister" gradually became accepted as the head of the government and its final authority. The prime minister chooses the members of his CABINET, consults with the GOVERNOR GENERAL, and decides on the date for an election; he takes personal responsibility for government policy and its success or failure. If he loses the support of his CAUCUS he will either be defeated in the House or forced to face a review of his leadership, and if he loses an election he will be pressured to resign as party leader. Between 1867 and 1990 Canada had seventeen prime ministers; some

served only a few months, others many years. All were either Conservative or Liberal and none was a woman. *See also*: GOVERNMENT, PMO, PRIVY COUNCIL.

Privilege

Because they meet under the symbolic protection of the Crown, Parliamentarians have special rights and freedoms not enjoyed by other citizens. The most important is freedom of speech: An MP or senator can say anything he pleases within the chamber or a committee room without fear of prosecution, but this protection does not extend to remarks made in the corridors or in press conferences. Parliamentarians are also excused from jury duty and may not be compelled to appear in court as witnesses. On Parliament Hill they are entitled to privacy (*see*: OASIS, OFFICE) and protection from threats, intimidation, and harrassment (*see*: SECURITY). They may also avoid arrest on the Hill while Parliament is sitting and for forty days before and after the session, but this freedom applies only to civil suits and not to criminal charges. It is a crime for any citizen to attempt to bribe, threaten, or influence a Parliamentarian's vote, and a crime for MPs and senators to take fees or favours in exchange for their political influence (*see*: CORRUPTION). Senators and MPs who are convicted of crimes usually resign, but they are not compelled to unless they are expelled by a majority vote of the house. In the nineteenth century, the Métis leader Louis Riel was twice elected in Manitoba and twice expelled for treason; in 1947 Communist MP Fred Rose was expelled after being convicted of espionage.

Privy Council Office

The administrative arm of the cabinet, the PCO has grown from a single clerk with a quill pen to a staff of more than four hundred headed by the most influential person in the Ottawa bureaucracy, the Clerk of the Privy Council. Records of cabinet meetings were rarely kept until the 1940s, now ministers can barely cope with the mountains of minutes and memoranda generated by the PCO. Although they work closely with the Prime Minister's Office, members of the PCO are public servants. They are expected to provide non-partisan advice, co-ordinate cabinet initiatives, and implement the objectives of the government,

The Privy Council Office or Cabinet Room in the East Block as it looked in the 1880s. Only a third of the present cabinet would be able to fit around this table.

although cabinet ministers sometimes feel that policy is being set by the PCO, not by themelves. *See also*: PMO, PRIME MINISTER.

Procedure

The business of Parliament is conducted according to a complex ritual of rules, traditions, and precedents. Rules are constantly changed or challenged, and new precedents are set by Speakers' rulings; knowledge of points of order and privilege, appropriate motions, and the limits and loopholes in the STANDING ORDERS is essential for a successful politician. A political party that masters the subtleties and strategems of procedure can stay in power a long time, or as the Opposition, hasten the government's defeat. It takes CLERKS decades to understand the nuances of the Parliamentary process, and few MPs ever acquire more than a basic knowledge of the rules of debate. Parliamentary procedure gives priority to government legislation, but it permits private members to introduce their own bills at specified times during the session, and it allows both private members and cabinet ministers to make brief statements before the daily debate begins. Precedence is given to COMMITTEE reports and PETITIONS from the public, and a specific time each day is allocated to QUESTION PERIOD. *See also*: DEBATE, SPEAKER, STANDING ORDERS, VOTE.

Progressive Conservative Party

One of Canada's oldest and most powerful political parties, the Conservatives, as they are usually called, formed Canada's first government in 1867 under Sir John A. Macdonald (1867-73, 1878-91). At that time, the party stood for loyalty to the Crown and Great Britain, economic nationalism, patriotism, and the extension of Canada to the Pacific Ocean by the Canadian Pacific Railroad. Conservative Prime Minister Sir Robert Borden (1911-20) established Canada's independence after the First World War, and Prime Minister R. B. Bennett (1930-35) led the country through the first half of the Great Depression. The word "Progressive" was added to the party's name in 1940, and Prime Minister John Diefenbaker (1957-63) liberalized the party by introducing populist ideas, a BILL OF RIGHTS, and votes for treaty Indians. In 1989, the Conservative government of Prime Minister Brian Mulroney (1984-) reversed the party's historic nationalism by adopting a free trade agreement with the United States, privatizing state corporations, and cutting financial support for railways and the Canadian Broadcasting Corporation. *See also*: LIBERAL PARTY, NEW DEMOCRATIC PARTY.

Prorogation

A session of Parliament can be frequently *adjourned* and it is *dissolved* for an election, but when the prime minister wants to make a fresh start with legislation without an election he *prorogues* Parliament. Prorogation ends the session, killing all proposed legislation not yet passed by the House of Commons and the Senate, and sets the date for the opening of next session. The new session can begin the very next day, and prorogation can take the form of a formal speech by the governor general, or a simple statement by the prime minister in the Commons. *See also*: OPENING.

Protocol

Canadians are a very relaxed, informal people, but state occasions demand ritualized behaviour that recognizes the power and status of the governor general, the prime minister, the chief justice, and the Speaker, as well as members of the diplomatic corps and foreign visitors. The rules of protocol are arcane and often hard to understand, but MPs must acquire at least a rudimentary knowledge of international good manners. It is no longer necessary to bow or curtsy to the Queen or the governor general, but no one says "Hi, how are ya?" to Her Majesty either. Formal dress is required on state occasions, and people are seated according to a pecking order of precedence that many of them take very seriously.

Provinces

Canada is made up of ten provinces and two territories: Newfoundland, Nova Scotia, Prince Edward Island, New Brunswick, Quebec, Ontario, Manitoba, Saskatchewan, Alberta, British Columbia, the Yukon Territory, and the

The wild rose, the official flower of the province of Alberta, is depicted in this stained-glass window in the west wall of the Commons chamber.

CANAPRESS

Northwest Territories. The provinces are self-governing, equal in status, and have some exclusive jurisdictions which are not shared with the federal government. The provinces are extremely unequal in size, population, wealth, and resources, as well as different in historical and cultural heritage (*see*: CONQUEST, UNITY), and one of the functions of the federal government is to equalize opportunities for all Canadians by redistributing money collected through taxes and by enforcing language laws and human rights in all provinces. Each province has its own legislature, with its own elected members, which is autonomous from the House of Commons; each territory has an elected council, but the council's decisions must be approved by a federal commissioner. Relations between the provinces, territories, and the federal government are often angry and argumentative, and seldom predictable.

Public

People get the government they deserve: the people of Canada ultimately govern themselves. However, in a Parliamentary system a government can win a majority of the seats in the House of Commons with a minority of the popular vote, leaving the majority of the population disgruntled and powerless. There is approximately one member of Parliament for every hundred thousand Canadians, and it is impossible for any MP to please all of the people all of the time; MPs are also pressured to vote according to their party's policy rather than the wishes of their constituents, and they almost always do. Public support depends on public opinion, which is known to be fickle, and politicians are constantly trying to shape public opinion and take the public's pulse through opinion polls.

Proceedings of the House of Commons are public (*see*: HANSARD, TELEVISION) but cabinet meetings, civil service proceedings, and many government documents are not (*see*: SECRECY). Politicians seek publicity for their achievements, but avoid publicizing their errors and indiscretions. The public may base its opinion on rumour and hearsay, but it is always right. *See also*: CONSTITUENCIES, ELECTION, GOVERNMENT

Public Service

See: CIVIL SERVICE.

Queen

Queen Elizabeth II is queen of Canada as well as queen of Great Britain and other nations of the British Commonwealth. The Queen is a frequent visitor to Canada. In 1957 and 1977 she read the Speech from the Throne at the

Queen Elizabeth II and her husband, Prince Philip, arrive with an escort of Royal Canadian Mounted Police to open Canada's Parliament in 1977.

CANAPRESS

Opening of the Canadian Parliament, and in 1982 she personally gave royal assent to the new Canadian Constitution in Ottawa. The Queen, her husband, Prince Philip, and other members of the Royal Family often open buildings and preside at sports competitions, exhibitions, and public functions across Canada. Royal visits are conducted with formal ceremony and arouse popular curiosity, but now that people of British origin are a minority in Canada, the Royal Family seems remote to many Canadians. The Queen is personally popular in English-speaking Canada, but in Quebec royal visits are opposed by French-Canadians who favour a sovereign Quebec. *See also*: CROWN, GOVERNOR GENERAL, UNITY.

Queen's Printer

All of the printing and publishing for Parliament and the Canadian government is the responsibility of the Queen's Printer, although 70 per cent is contracted out to private companies. For the House of Commons and the Senate, the Queen's Printer produces bills and reports, the daily Order Paper, office stationery, bulletins, and labels, as well as the daily JOURNALS and HANSARD. Copies of all public documents are available for free or for a nominal charge. The first Queen's Printer, George Edward Desbarats, was hired in 1869; his office was made a government department in 1886.

Question Period

The right to question the government is one of the most cherished rights in a free society, and every day of the session the House of Commons sets aside forty-five minutes for questions from the MPs. Monday to Thursday, Question Period starts at 2:15 p.m., Fridays at 11:15 a.m. Questions are usually related to the controversies of the day and are designed to embarrass a cabinet minister or to catch him out in a mistake; in reply, the minister attempts to make the questioner look like a fool. The verbal swordplay can be witty and sometimes vicious, but Question Period is usually a noisy shouting match with questions often drowned out by bellowing MPs. Canadians find Question Period exciting television, and some MPs become popular because of their theatrical performances. Some people mistakenly think that the disorderly style of Question Period governs all debate in the House; others wish it did. In fact, most questions are not asked verbally during Question Period but are submitted in writing to the CLERK who places them on the ORDERS OF THE DAY. The minister may respond to these questions verbally or in writing. *See also*: LATE SHOW, TELEVISION.

Quorum

Only twenty MPs are required to be present in the House of Commons chamber for debate to take place. As a result, the chamber is frequently virtually empty. *See also*: COMMITTEES.

R

Reading Room

The FIRE of 1916 started in the Reading Room of the original Centre Block, and when the building was rebuilt, the most important room, next to the Commons chamber itself, was the Reading Room next door. In this bright, high-ceilinged room, members of Parliament could browse through hundreds of newspapers and journals from around the world or bury themselves in popular

The Reading Room as it was in the 1920s.

NATIONAL ARCHIVES OF CANADA / PA-34213

novels, and in the days when MPs' offices were cramped and uncomfortable the Reading Room offered a quiet escape. The first Reading Room had been intended to be a picture gallery, and the walls of the new room were decorated with a series of large murals by Arthur Crisp depicting the importance of printing; the heads of ten prominent Canadian journalists are carved in stone beneath the arches of the short corridor leading to the Hall of Honour. In 1990 the Reading Room was converted into a committee meeting room, and the new reading room was relegated to a small, windowless space in the basement. See also: LIBRARY, STONE CARVING, TELEVISION.

Red

The traditional colour of the British CROWN, red is the official colour of the SENATE, or Red chamber, a reflection of its origins in the HOUSE OF LORDS. The Senate chamber and its public rooms have red carpets, Senate documents are published in red bindings, and some senators decorate their offices with red leather sofas and red wallpaper. Red is also the colour of the LIBERAL PARTY. The PROGRESSIVE CONSERVATIVE PARTY's colour is blue, and the NDP can't make up its mind. *See also:* GREEN.

Renovation

Because of their age and heavy use, as well as the ravages of Ottawa weather, the buildings of the Parliamentary precinct are continually being rebuilt, restored, rewired, and repainted. Styles have frequently changed over 125 years, and the architecture and history of Parliament Hill have not always been respected. In 1960, the interior of the West Block was gutted to create modern office space that completely destroyed the building's Victorian interior; renovators ripped out an entire floor to create the vast Confederation Room – Room 200 – where receptions are held, and a cafeteria and kitchen were built in the central open courtyard, ensuring that the smell of cooking grease would permeate the entire building (*see:* FRENCH FRIES). In 1980 an elevator was added to the Peace Tower and the observation deck was glassed in to prevent people from jumping

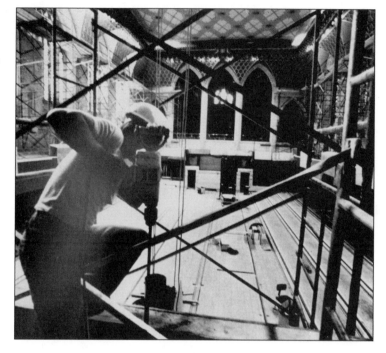

Nothing is permanent in politics; and an MP often finds himself without a seat.

CANAPRESS

to their deaths or hurling bombs at the prime minister (*see:* BOMB, LAVATORIES, SECURITY). In the late 1980s the upper floors of the monumental Wellington Building were redone in a peculiar shade of mauve that later spread to the Victoria Building; mauve was an improvement on the indigestion-yellow of the West Block, and they may eventually get the elevators in the Wellington Building to work.

Between 1867 and 1967 almost all the original Victorian furnishings on Parliament Hill were thrown out or carted off by souvenir hunters. Almost everything in the Centre Block was lost in the FIRE of 1916, but the later destruction was deliberate. "It is difficult to comprehend the cheerful vandalism of successive generations," writes R. A. J. Phillips of the fate of the East Block following the Second World War. "The main entranceway, under the Southwest Tower, was gutted and fitted with oak doorways styled after fashionable suburbia. The elegant cage elevator was torn out for the modern grace of concrete block walls. The governor general's entrance was cemented up to accomodate a bureaucrat in suitable splendor. The main corridor, terminating in a Gothic window, was blocked off for an office. Fireplaces were eliminated with jackhammers. Washbasins, which once gave near godliness to the offices of senior officials, were yanked out; a couple were saved when, according to legend, the occupants chained themselves to the plumbing."

Between 1967 and 1976, $15 million was spent to renovate and restore the East Block. Much of the early vandalism was undone; staircases were reopened, marble fireplaces stripped of their paint, and the garish institutional lighting replaced by antique fixtures in the hallways. Four offices were restored to their colourful Victorian magnificence and their original furnishings retrieved from attics and warehouses. These offices are not in use and are open to public tours on weekends; some private offices retain their original wood panelling, but only the Library looks almost exactly as it did originally. *See also*: EAST BLOCK, FIRE, LIBRARY, OFFICES, TOURS, WEST BLOCK.

Research

A hundred years ago MPs and senators kept themselves informed by reading newspapers and magazines and by cultivating a large personal acquaintance among influential people in business and public life. Voters looked to their MPs to inform them about government policy, and MPs were expected to make speeches of an hour or more based on their personal knowledge of complex issues. Today MPs and senators have professional researchers to dig up their information and draft their speeches. Most of the researchers are hired by the political parties: each party receives a financial stipend from the House of Commons to cover research expenses. Research assistance is also provided free by the LIBRARY OF PARLIAMENT, where a staff of impartial and expert researchers will supply detailed information and position papers on any topic an MP or senator requests. Library researchers will also analyze the information and if requested will offer various interpretations according to the politician's political bias. Perhaps it is coincidence, but as MPs' expertise has increased, their ideological differences have become less pronounced.

Restaurants

In addition to the Parliamentary DINING ROOM, Parliament Hill has six cafeterias and snack bars and three small private dining rooms. Most popular with the staff is the West Block cafeteria, where security guards gossip with secretaries and reporters are tipped off by political aides while everyone strains to overhear a juicy tidbit. The food is fast, fried, and cheap, the room crowded, and the noise loud. The restaurants are busiest in the winter when the weather keeps people indoors; in summer they lose business to the hotdog and chip wagons on Sparks Street (*see*: FRENCH FRIES). MPs and senators tend to be picky eaters, suspicious of exotic, ethnic, or experimental cooking and fond of back-home favourites such as meat loaf, roast beef, and macaroni and cheese. They like their food to look like what it is, and while salads and muffins are gaining popularity, the full-course, meat-and-potatoes meal is still standard. Some MPs and many staff members bring brown-bag lunches and eat in their offices. Parliament runs on coffee: the restaurants serve an averge of fifty thousand cups a month.

Rideau Hall

The official residence of the governor general, Rideau Hall was built in 1832 as a private home for a wealthy contractor, Thomas MacKay. It has been enlarged and modernized over the years, and now contains office space for the governor general's staff as well as living quarters for his family. When the Queen or other members of the Royal Family visit Ottawa they stay at Rideau Hall or at the guest house, 7 Rideau Gate. Rideau Hall was once the sports and social centre of Ottawa. It had a curling rink and skating rink, a toboggan slide, and a theatre in the ballroom; fancy dress balls, banquets, and teas at Rideau Hall provided the principal entertainment for politicians during the months when Parliament was in session. Cricket is still played on the grounds, which are open to the public. Group tours of the public rooms may be arranged on request, and in the summer the members of the Governor General's Foot Guard and the Grenadier Guards perform a changing of the guard ceremony similar to Buckingham Palace's. *See also*: CHANGING OF THE GUARD, GOVERNOR GENERAL.

The front entrance to Rideau Hall.

NCC/CCN

The Tent Room in Rideau Hall arranged for a banquet. It was built by an early governor general as a tennis court and games room.

NCC/CCN

Riding

See: CONSTITUENCY

Rotunda

Formally named Confederation Hall, the circular, vaulted rotunda inside the main entrance to the Centre Block links the Commons wing on the west to the Senate wing on the east. The rotunda is the main meeting place on the Hill, and during the day it is buzzing with activity. Guided tours start on the east side of the rotunda, and other visitors must check in at a security desk on the west side. The walls of the rotunda are Tyndall limestone from Manitoba, the pillars are black marble, and the floor is black and white marble set in a wavy, circular pattern that sug-

Beneath the medieval gothic pillars of the rotunda, a modern security guard keeps watch.

PAUL VON BAICH

gests the sea. The central column is carved with an allegorical figure of Neptune, and its base is set with a sixteen-point mariner's compass or *rose des vents*.

Royal Assent

No bill becomes law until it has received royal assent and been signed by the governor general as well as the prime minister. Royal assent is given at a quaint ceremony in the Senate usually presided over by a judge of the Supreme Court acting for the governor general, and several bills are normally assented to at one ceremony. The judge arrives at the Senate just prior to the end of a day's sitting, and when he has taken his place on the throne, the Gentleman Usher of the BLACK ROD goes down the hall to the Commons chamber where he knocks three times on the door to summon the MPs to the ceremony. The MPs troop down the hall and take their places at the BAR of the Senate, much as they do at the Opening of Parliament. The Clerk Assistant of the Senate reads the title of each bill aloud in both English and French, and when the Clerk of the Senate says, "In Her Majesty's name, the Honourable the Deputy of His Excellency the Governor General doth assent to these Bills," the judge nods his head. When the bill involves spending public money, the exclusive jurisdiction of the Commons, the judge in the name of the Queen "thanks her loyal subjects, accepts their benevolence, and assents to this Bill." Financial bills are personally handed to the Clerk of the Senate by the Speaker of the House of Commons and are distinguished by a green ribbon. Royal assent is never refused. *See also*: ACT, BILL.

Royal Canadian Mounted Police

Famous for their scarlet coats, stetsons, and high leather boots, the Mounties are a popular symbol of Canada, yet except for special occasions such as the OPENING of Parliament, they are more likely to be plainly dressed in parkas or windbreakers and navy blue trousers with a yellow stripe up the side. The RCMP police the grounds of Parliament Hill but they are not permitted inside the Parliament Buildings without the permission of the Speaker (*see*: PRIVILEGE). Outside the Parliament buildings, the RCMP are responsible for the personal safety of the prime minister

This cheerful cutout may be the only scarlet-coated Mountie most visitors to Parliament Hill will ever see.

PAUL VON BAICH

and his family, the governor general, and any MPs or senators whose lives may be threatened. *See also*: SECURITY.

Rules

See: STANDING ORDERS

S

Salaries

In 1991, a member of Parliament was paid $64,400 a year, plus a tax-free allowance of $27,300 and a senator the same salary plus $10,100 for expenses; the Speakers, cabinet ministers, Parliamentary secretaries, party leaders, and party whips receive additional bonuses. Although the MPs receive many free benefits (*see*: PERKS) they also face extra personal expenses: most maintain two residences, one in Ottawa and one in their constituency, they are expected to entertain their supporters, and they have to dress presentably. MPs who serve six years or more receive lifetime pensions scaled to their years of service and their salary levels. In addition to his salary, an MP receives $165,000 a year to operate his offices in Ottawa and in his constituency. *See also*: BUDGET, OFFICES, SENATE.

Scandal

The most effective way to damage or destroy an MP's political career is to embroil him in a scandal. Scandals often involve sex: in the late 1950s, one cabinet minister became involved with a German prostitute believed to be a spy. Private members are occasionally accused of sexual harrassment or discovered in embarrassing predicaments: one MP engaged in an office *amour* accidentally locked himself out of his office wearing only a House of Commons' towel. Scandals also involve theft, abuse of Parliamentary privileges, lying to the House, accepting bribes in return for favours, associating with criminals, using public money for private business, interfering with a criminal investigation, or attempting to influence the courts. Scandals are relatively rare and often trivial but they make a strong impression on voters and can lead to the defeat of a government. *See also*: CORRUPTION, GOSSIP.

Scrum

Reporters are not content simply to report what is said in the House of Commons, and while the prime minister or a controversial MP can escape the press in his office or in the Commons chamber, reporters and television cameramen gather in the hall or Commons foyer to accost ministers coming out of cabinet meetings or debates. When their victim finally emerges, the mob of shouting, shoving reporters resembles a ball toss, or scrum, in an English rugby game. Scrums usually happen at 3:00 p.m. following QUESTION PERIOD, and the scrum is a major feature of the television evening news. A politician's prestige is measure by the size and frequency of his scrums, although he often has very little to say in all the hubbub. Scrum is also used as a verb, as in "to scrum" or "to be scrummed."

Prime Minister Brian Mulroney in the midst of a scrum in 1991.

MONE CHENG PHOTOGRAPHY STUDIO

Sculpture

See: STONE CARVING

Secrecy

Until the eighteenth century, the proceedings of the British House of Commons were conducted in the deepest secrecy, largely in order to prevent individual members from being murdered or arrested for treason because of critical remarks they made in debate. Voters had no way of knowing what their representatives were doing unless the MPs chose to tell them, and no way of verifying it. As the power of the Lords and religious denominations waned and the printing press made information easily available, MPs began leaking accounts of House proceedings to friendly journalists. These accounts were biased and garbled, and the House came to accept the fact that not only should accurate records of debates be published (*see*: HANSARD) but independent reporters should be allowed to hear the debates. While it is now accepted in principle that the proceedings of the House are public, cabinet meetings are still secret, and debates can be closed to the public if there is a threat to security. Governments generally believe that the less the public knows, the better. *See also*: PRESS GALLERY, SECURITY, STRANGERS.

Secretaries

There are two kinds of secretaries on Parliament Hill, Parliamentary secretaries and secretaries who type letters and answer phones. Parliamentary secretaries are elected MPs of the government party appointed by the prime minister to assist senior cabinet ministers. Parliamentary secretaries undertake many of the minor chores of the minister's job, answer questions on his behalf in the House, and learn the intricacies of preparing legislation in the hope they too will one day make it into the cabinet. Parliamentary secretaries have considerably higher status than the other secretaries, who are hired by the MPs and senators, yet after many years working on the Hill some private secretaries become knowledgable and powerful players behind the scenes. MPs were not given secretarial help until 1913, and then only on a part-time basis. Full-time secretaries were first allowed in 1968. *See also*: OFFICES, STAFF.

Security

The Sergeant-at-Arms with his mace has multiplied into a security staff of more than two hundred that guards the House of Commons day and night; the Senate has its own security staff and senators' office desks are equipped with secret "panic buttons" to summon help. The prime minister's office and cabinet room on the third floor are roped off and guarded; the Senate and Commons chambers are inspected before each day's sitting. Details of security precautions are not published, and guards attempt to maintain an open, friendly atmosphere

Parliamentary security guards: Left? Right?

BREGG/CANAPRESS

while keeping a sharp eye out for trouble. All of the House of Commons and Senate buildings are closed to the public except for the PUBLIC GALLERIES and the few rooms shown during guided TOURS. Appointments to see MPs must be made in advance by mail or telephone, and all visitors have to be issued a pass. Security is designed to protect the MP's privacy as well as his life: no one wants to open his office door to find disgruntled constituents camped out in the hall. *See also*: BOMB, DEMONSTRATIONS, RCMP.

Senate

Often called the "chamber of sober second thought," the Senate is Canada's "upper house," a substitute for the British HOUSE OF LORDS. No BILL can become law in Canada unless it is passed by both the Senate and the HOUSE OF COMMONS, and bills originate in both houses. The Senate does not have the power to introduce bills involving the raising or spending of money, and the majority of all legislation originates with the Commons. Senators are appointed by the prime minister and serve until the age of seventy-five; a senator must be over thirty years of age, a resident of the province he represents, and the owner of debt-free property worth at least $4,000. There are normally 104 senators, although there may be as many as twenty vacant seats, and the prime minister has the power to appoint more; in 1990 the number of senators was temporarily raised to 112 so the government could ensure that a controversial tax bill would pass the Senate.

The Senate was intended to ensure balanced representation for all regions of Canada regardless of population. Ontario, Quebec, the four western provinces together, and the three eastern provinces together, each have twenty-four senators; Newfoundland has six, and each of the two territories has one. However, since they are political appointees, senators tend to represent their political parties more than their regions, and Senate votes are generally split down party lines. Since all prime ministers have been Liberal or Conservative, the Senate remains a two-party house with almost no minority party representation and only a handful of Independents. The property requirement established the

The Senate can be passionate and rambunctious place. In 1990 the media were invited into the Senate chamber to cover a noisy fracas between Liberal and Conservative senators.

CANAPRESS

Senate as a house of the wealthy middle class, and senators remain unrepresentative of the Canadian population, although the proportion of women, one in six, is slightly higher than in the House of Commons. Until 1965 senators were appointed for life; their average age was over seventy and many were too old and ill to attend regularly. Now the average age is sixty-one and the Senate is a much more vocal and vigorous body.

The Senate meets only three afternoons a week, Tuesday to Thursday, although senators, like MPs, spend a great deal of time in COMMITTEES and attend CAUCUS meetings of their parties. Some senators are also cabinet ministers, including the leader of the government party in the Senate, who introduces bills from the House of Commons and leads the debate. PROCEDURE in the Senate is similar to the House of Commons'; bills are read, studied, amended and voted on. All amendments have to be approved by the House of Commons, and the Senate is expected to pass bills already passed by the Commons. It usually does, although senators who dislike a bill can resort to procedural tactics and FILIBUSTERS to delay it in the hope the session will end and the bill will die; some bills are tied up in

Senate committees for months. Conceived as a moderating influence, the Senate can become obstructive when Liberal and Conservative senators are almost equal in number, or when government senators are outnumbered by opposition senators, and in 1990 the Senate erupted in riotous behaviour over the unpopular tax bill.

Because senators are not accountable to the public in elections, the Senate is not popular with Canadians. There are continual proposals to reform it or abolish it, and while many senators bring a wealth of wisdom and experience to their jobs, generations of prime ministers have used Senate appointments to reward faithful party hacks and wealthy bagmen whose contribution to government has often been nil. Senators who go bankrupt or are convicted of crimes do not have to resign unless the Senate votes to expel them, although most do. The Senate costs TAXPAYERS about $43 million a year. In 1991 each senator was paid $64,400 plus a tax free allowance of $10,100. Senators also get offices, secretaries, and many other PERKS, including messenger service and access to the LIBRARY and parliamentary DINING ROOM. The Senate controls its own administrative budget and has its own staff of CLERKS, MESSENGERS, and SECURITY GUARDS.

Senators have more individual freedom of speech than do members of Parliament. Government business is not necessarily given precedence in the Senate, and on forty-eight-hours notice a senator can initiate a debate on any matter of public concern; the debate has no time limit, and no vote is automatically taken. Senators address each other directly by name, not through the SPEAKER as in the House of Commons, and rulings by the Speaker can be overturned by a vote of the senators. Senators can speak as long as they like; there is no set time for daily adjournment and no closure (*see*: DEBATE). The Senate's QUESTION PERIOD also has no time limit. Debate in the Senate can go on indefinitely unless the senators themselves decide to call a vote. While this freedom allows senators to be longwinded and irrelevant, it also enables them to introduce concerns that MPs might find politically unattractive, and the Senate has taken the initiative investigating areas such as illiteracy and consumer affairs. Many senators remain active in business and the professions and work very hard behind the scenes on party organization and public policy. *See also*: HOUSE OF COMMONS

Sergeant-at-Arms

At one time the king's personal bodyguard, the Sergeant-at-Arms carries the MACE to guard the SPEAKER from harm as he enters and leaves the Commons chamber and stations himself just inside main door when the House of Commons is sitting. He is responsible for the security of the House of Commons precinct and the personal safety of the members. He has the authority to remove both MPs and spectators who behave in a disorderly way, and when the Senate wishes to communicate formally with the Commons, the Gentleman Usher of the BLACK ROD must get the permission of the Sergeant-at-Arms to enter the Commons chamber. A professional military officer, the Sergeant-at-Arms wears a black uniform with a cocked hat that symbolizes his historic role. *See also:* SPEAKER, STAFF.

Carrying the mace, Sergeant-at-Arms Major-General M. G. Cloutier leads Speaker Jeanne Sauvé into the Commons chamber in 1982.

MITCHELL / CANAPRESS

Session

A session of Parliament in the nineteenth century used to last about four months, from February to May. Now it usually lasts a year, although it may last two or more years. A session is frequently adjourned to enable MPs to spend time in their constituencies and to vacation, and it may be PROROGUED to allow the government to start a new session with a Speech from the Throne. There are usually three or four sessions before Parliament is dissolved for an election.

Sitting

The House of Commons sits five days a week while it is in session, the Senate three days (*see*: HOURS). Until 1982 the Commons sat at night, sometimes until 3:00 a.m. or 4:00 a.m. Emergency or closured debates are still permitted in the evening, but debate now adjourns by midnight.

Sound-and-Light Show

Every night during July and August and four nights a week during May and June, Parliament Hill is illuminated for a half-hour sound-and-light show featuring dramatic events and characters from Canadian history. Two shows are given every night, one in English, one in French, starting at 9:30 p.m. *See also*: INFORMATION, TOURISTS.

Speaker

Literally the member of Parliament who speaks on behalf of all members of the House of Commons, the Speaker was originally appointed by the king and later by the prime minister. The Speaker of the Senate is still appointed, but in 1986 the Speaker of the House of Commons was elected in a free vote of all MPs. The Commons Speaker has a great deal of responsibility: several British Speakers were executed for bearing bad news to the king, and one Canadian Speaker went mad – he also shot rabbits from his office window on Parliament Hill. Whatever the Speaker's own political convictions, he must be fair and

Workmen install a hydraulic life under the seat of the Speaker's chair so a short Speaker may comfortably rise to the occasion.

DAVE BUSTON / CANAPRESS

impartial in giving MPs of all parties the right to speak; the Speaker does not vote except to break a tie. He must keep ORDER during DEBATE and interpret the rules of procedure when his authority is challenged. In recognition of his authority, the Speaker is given an impressive chair on a dias at the north end of the CHAMBER. The chair has a intricately carved wooden canopy and is equipped with a hydraulic lift so that short Speakers can elevate themselves to command a view of the House. The chair also has a microphone and speakers to enable the Speaker to hear and be heard, and a control that enables him to switch off all the MPs' microphones. Lights in the canopy shine on the writing surfaces of the armrests, and the arms contain storage compartments for books and papers. Inscribed on the left side of the chair are four Latin mottos to encourage the Speaker in his work: "Neither by entreaty nor gifts," "Liberty lies in the laws," "Envy is the enemy of honour," and "Praise be to God." Three more mottos are inscribed on the right: "The hand that deals justly is a sweet-smelling ointment," "Mindful and faithful," and "A mind conscious of the right." Until 1921, when this chair was presented to the House of Commons by the British branch of the Empire Parliamentary Association, Speakers took their chairs home with them on retirement.

In keeping with his historic role, the Speaker wears a costume derived from court dress: a tricorn hat, black suit, white collar with tabs, black silk robe, and white gloves, although in the British House of Commons the Speaker also wears

The Speaker of the House of Commons, John Fraser, in his office in 1988. The chandelier has been replaced since 1931, and the buffalo hides are gone.

a white wig, lace ruffles, and buckled shoes. At the start of each day's sitting the Speaker's parade marches from the Speaker's office down the HALL OF HONOUR to the FOYER and the Commons chamber. Led by the Chief Constable and two officers, the SERGEANT-AT-ARMS carries the MACE in front of the Speaker, who is followed by a page, the CLERK, and the assistant clerks. The parade has no purpose and takes only a few minutes, but it adds a touch of theatre to the proceedings.

The Speaker is also the head housekeeper of the Commons. He chairs the BOARD OF INTERNAL ECONOMY, which is responsible for a BUDGET of more than $230 million and the efficient running of the Commons PRECINCT. As the representative of the House of Commons, the Speaker attends international meetings of parliamentarians, speaks to public service organizations, and entertains a wide variety of dignitaries and celebrities, from visiting royalty to Olympic athletes. For this purpose he has a private DINING ROOM next to his office. Between 1867 and 1916 the Speaker's family lived in a suite of rooms in the north wing of the Centre Block (*see*: FIRE) but they now live at Kingsmere in a house that used to be the summer residence of Prime Minister Mackenzie King.

In addition the Speaker maintains a dressing room in his Centre Block office and a tiny two-room apartment with a hideway bed for nights when he is kept late in the House. The Speaker is paid a substantial bonus and provided with many PERKS, including a chauffeured limousine, but he earns his keep: his day often begins at 7:00 a.m. and ends after midnight. When the Speaker is not in the chair, his place is taken by the Deputy Speaker, who also presides over the House when it sits as a committee. "Speakers must be authoritative without being overbearing; dignified but not lacking in wit or humour and capable of maintaining a distance from other members without appearing aloof," Gary Levy writes in *Speakers of the House of Commons*. "General elections pose a special dilemma for the Speaker. Having sought to establish and maintain a reputation for impartiality, the Speaker faces the prospect of either running as an independent or seeking the nomination of a political party. The former choice may expose him to defeat, the latter may jeopardize his ability to continue in the Chair." *See also*: DEBATE, DECORUM, NAMING, PROCEDURE, SENATE, UNPARLIAMENTARY.

Speech

An MP's stature used to be judged by his ability to make a brilliant speech in the House of Commons. Prime ministers and cabinet ministers commonly spoke for four or five hours in important debates, and speeches regularly ran an hour or more. MPs would spend weeks working up and memorizing their speeches – it is still improper to read aloud any speech except the budget – larding their rhetoric with appropriate quotations from Shakespeare or Plato. Speeches were reported verbatim in the local newspapers, giving the voters an accurate idea of what MPs were saying on their behalf. Time limits and TELEVISION have made a speeches a lost art. Prime ministers now rarely speak in the House except at QUESTION PERIOD, and elsewhere their speeches are "ghosted" by professional speechwriters. An MP's first speech is called a maiden speech and usually consists of platitudes about the MP's own riding, all of which are greeted politely by the opposition. Some MPs never make a speech at all. *See also*: DEBATE, PROCEDURE.

A session is over, the MPs have gone, and the staff cleans out their desks in the Commons chamber.

BREGG/CANAPRESS

Staff

For every MP or senator on Parliament Hill, there are eight more people hired to grease the wheels of the Parliamentary machine. With a combined staff of about three thousand, the Hill is a small town where people are in constant communication and where rivalries between departments are more cutthroat than anything that happens in Parliament. Elected MPs come and go, but the staff stays on for years, providing secure, traditional continuity and a highly ritualized way of life. Parliament still resembles a medieval guild where apprentices are trained from an early age, promoted by seniority, and everyone gets ahead by obeying the rules. A new BACKBENCHER soon learns that whatever the folks at home may expect, his happiness on the Hill will depend on his willingness to follow the advice of the clerks and the Sergeant-at-Arms and on his ability to make friends with the secretaries, messengers, carpenters, and the executive chef. So complete are the services available to MPs and senators that the Hill is almost self-sufficient: the staff includes curators and cleaners, accountants, aides and auditors, lawyers, librarians, television producers, printers, cooks, upholsterers, translators, drycleaners, and waitresses. The size of the House of Commons staff increased so rapidly between 1970 and 1980 that no one really knew who was working on the Hill or what they were doing there; a critical report by the auditor general brought a brisk housecleaning and a reduction in the size of the staff. In 1991 the auditor general suggested that the Senate could also do with some housecleaning, and the Senate complied. Messengers are being replaced by computers or postal service, but the Parliament Buildings are still so crowded that during a session it's impossible to find a nook or cranny without somebody in it. Perhaps coincidentally, this feeling of teeming human life is a characteristic of the Gothic architecture of the buildings themselves.

Stained Glass

The chamber of the House of Commons has twelve of the most beautiful stained-glass windows to be found anywhere in Canada. Designed by government sculptor Eleanor Milne and crafted by Toronto artist Russell Goodman between 1968 and 1973, the windows depict the official flowers of each of the ten provinces and two territories, starting on the west wall with the white dogwood of British Columbia and ending on the east wall with Newfoundland's pitcher plant. The windows depicting the fireweed of the Yukon and mountain avens of the Northwest Territories are appropriately on the north wall of the chamber behind the public gallery. The windows incorporate the traditional leaf and fern patterns of Gothic design, and one of the the most striking is the brilliant red orange of the Saskatchewan tiger lily in the centre of the west wall. Stained-glass windows depicting allegorical figures of War and Peace also decorate the MEMORIAL CHAMBER, and the Commons' FOYER has an etched-

Detail of a stained-glass window.

PAUL VON BAICH

glass ceiling that includes panels showing government departmens, including Finance, Agriculture, and Fisheries.

Standing Orders

Procedure in the House of Commons is governed by 159 rules or Standing Orders. These rules govern the presentation of motions, the length of debate, the conduct of members, and the order of business of the Commons. The Standing Orders are always being questioned, ignored, and revised, and their enforcement and interpretation is established by decades of precedent and custom. *See also*: CLERK, PROCEDURE, SPEAKER.

Statues

Canada's most famous and revered prime ministers have been cast in bronze and their statues placed at strategic points on Parliament Hill. The statues form an interesting focal point for summer walking TOURS, and they include early political heros such as Thomas D'Arcy McGee and George Brown, both by sculptor George Hill. Sir John A. Macdonald stands just to the west of the Centre Block, near his Quebec colleague Sir George-Etienne Cartier and his Liberal opponent Alexander Mackenzie, all designed by Quebec sculptor Louis-Phillippe Hébert. Sir Wilfrid Laurier is on the east side of the Hill in front of the East Block, looking towards Quebec and the hotel that bears his name, and his Conservative rival, Sir Robert Borden, strikes a combative pose near the West Block facing Wellington Street. Laurier, by Montreal sculptor Joseph-Emile Brunet, is shown in a characteristic casual pose, one hand on hip, as if addressing the House of Commons, whereas Borden's statue, by Frances Loring of Toronto, reflects his position as Canada's prime minister during the First World War. The statue of Canada's longest serving prime minister, William Lyon Mackenzie King, stands near the northwest corner of the East Block, close to where his office was for twenty-two years, and the scowling, squint-eyed, buttoned-up figure by Quebec artist Reoul Hunter admirably captures King's repressed, suspicious personality. The statue of Prime Minister John Diefenbaker by Leo Mol of Winnipeg, standing to the west of the Centre Block, one hand in his pocket, is equally evocative of Diefenbaker's aggressive personality, as is the casual, smiling figure of Lester Pearson seated on the hill behind. A massive bronze figure of Louis St. Laurent by Vancouver sculptor Elek Imredy sits in front of the Supreme Court of Canada just to the west of Parliament Hill on

The statue of Queen Victoria on a knoll west of the Centre Block. The British lion looks more virile than he is.

NCC/CCN

Wellington Street Also on Wellington, near the corner of Metcalfe, is a romantic statue of Sir Galahad erected in memory of a young civil servant, Bert Harper, who drowned in the Ottawa River on December 6, 1901, when he tried to rescue a skater, Bessie Blair, who had fallen through the ice. The statue, by American Ernest Keyser, was paid for by a public subscription organized by Harper's friend, the future prime minister Mackenzie King. A bronze statue of an MP killed in the First World War, Lieutenant-Colonel George Baker, is in the House of Commons foyer.

Not all prime ministers have made it to the Hill. The grotesquely elongated sculpture of Conservative Arthur Meighen was rejected, in the words of John Diefenbaker, as "the greatest monstrosity ever produced, a mixture of Ichabod Crane and Daddy Longlegs," and the stylized pink-marble statue of R. B. Bennett was dismissed as "a mummy." Both remain in a warehouse, while the living prime ministers and those who served a brief time have not been commemorated.

The dominant statue on the Hill is a regal figure of young Queen Victoria on a pedestal, which stands west of the Centre Block. Designed after her death in 1901 by Louis-Phillippe Hébert, the base of the statue features a second female figure representing Canada and a haughty, muscular British lion. After the statue was erected in 1908, it was discovered that the lion's rampant pose made British virility all too obvious, especially to curious children, and the lion's sexual organs were removed. The scar where the incision was made can be clearly seen today.

Stone Carvers

When architect John Pearson designed the new Centre Block in 1916, he hired stone carvers to decorate the interior and exterior of the building with GARGOYLES, heraldic motifs, fabulous beasts, and the luxuriant foliage patterns characteristic of the Gothic style. During construction, Pearson employed from four to seven carvers under superintendent Walter Allen for an average of $1 to $1.50 an hour. They carved the animal groups on the gables of the ground-floor windows showing wolves, beavers, bear, and buffalo, as well as sixteen gargoyles and the GROTESQUES of two architects, Pearson and Thomas Fuller, beside the main door. The limestone heads of twenty prominent politicians peer down from the Commons FOYER, humourous and realistic down to their moustaches and eyeglasses. The exterior figures were denounced as "mudpie faces" and "disgusting jokes in stone" by the superindentent of art for Ottawa schools.

In 1926 American sculptor Ira Lake was hired to carve the interior of the MEMORIAL CHAMBER, but the first full-time official carver, Cleophas Soucy, was not permanently employed until 1948. Soucy had worked under Allen and Lake and was given his own assistant, Coeur-de-Lion MacCarthy. Between 1936 and

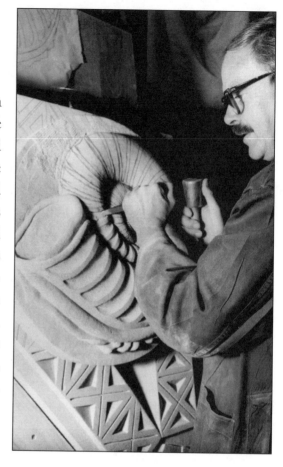

Carver Maurice Joanisse chisels a detail for a stone frieze.

PAUL VON BAICH

1939 Soucy and his team of thirteen carvers completed the carving in the Senate chamber and the large lion and unicorn at the entrance to the peace tower. With the outbreak of the Second World War, the carving program was suspended and not begun again until 1947 when Soucy completed ten heads of Press Gallery journalists in the hall-way leading to the READING ROOM. In 1950 Soucy was succeeded by William Oosterhoff, who carved the frieze around the ceiling of the Commons FOYER depicting the floral emblems and leading industries of the provinces – the heads of a miner, logger, farmer, and fisherman occupy the four corners. In 1962 Eleanor Milne became the third official stone carver. Skilled also at drawing and design, Milne's impact on the House of Commons has been dramatic. Between 1962 and 1975 Milne and her team of carvers created the ten-panel, 120-foot History of Canada frieze around the gallery in the Commons foyer, working at night so the noise of their pneumatic tools would not disturb debate. During this time she also designed and supervised the construction of twelve STAINED-GLASS windows for the Commons CHAMBER. Between 1975 and 1985 Milne directed a team of carvers led by Christopher Fairbrother in the creation of twelve stone panels for the Commons chamber depicting the Constitution, and in 1986 she designed a series of smaller carvings for the

Eleanor Milne, Dominion Sculptress 1962-92, wears goggles to protect her eyes from limestone dust.

GEORGE WILKES / HOUSE OF COMMONS COLLECTIONS

chamber depicting the evolution of life; these were carved by Maurice Joanisse. In 1978 nine Native and Inuit carvers were assigned to create panels for the door lintels in the Commons foyer.

Milne's team worked on a scaffold in the foyer to carve the History of Canada panels, but in later projects the stones were removed from the wall and carved in a workshop on Somerset Street. Unlike earlier carvers, who made maquettes of their designs, Milne drew directly on the stone from preliminary sketches. The stone is gouged out and back-cut behind each figure to make the carving stand out, and the contrast becomes greater as the carving ages or weathers.

Stone Carvings

The motifs of Gothic carving are organic and humanistic: flowers, foliage, birds, animals, and people are all entwined in sinuous patterns based on natural shapes. While the figures are realistic, they are often distorted or exaggerated, and mythical animals such as unicorns and griffons are mixed in with lions and beavers. The carvings in the Parliament Buildings represent more than thirty different animals, including squirrels and mountain goats, lobsters and crabs, bats, toads, and turtles. Even dragonflies and butterflies have not been forgotten, and some distinctly Canadian pine-cones have been included among the traditional roses, lilies, and shamrocks; the Native carvers have depicted fish, seals, and killer whales. The original Gothic designs have also been updated to include airplanes, tractors, and hydro generators, and the more recent carvings

The scaffold on the right is where Eleanor Milne worked at night to carve the stone frieze above the arches of the Commons foyer.

CANAPRESS

show the influence of modern Impressionist and Inuit styles. The Gothic style is particularly suited to Parliament because it is democratic: it portrays ordinary, homely people wearing everyday working clothes, and it often makes fun of people by exaggerating their faults. The unpopular King Edward VIII, who abdicated in 1936, is carved in the Senate foyer with bulging eyes and a bulbous nose, and the ugly, grimacing faces of many famous politicians have startled and amused generations of visitors to the Hill: carver Oosterhof even added his own smiling face to the stone crowd in the Senate foyer.

The struggles of Canada's first settlers form the theme of Eleanor Milne's stone frieze in the Commons foyer depicting the history of Canada from prehistoric times to the arrival of the United Empire Loyalists in the eighteenth century, and Milne incorporates modern images such as a railroad to link the past with the present. In her twelve allegorical stone panels in the Commons chamber depicting various aspects of the Constitution, Milne has included an accident between a car and a bicycle in the panel on Civil Law, and a whale in the Taxation panel symbolizes a growing concern with the environment. The practice of including living people is no longer followed–subjects must be dead at least fifty years– and the striking absence of women, children, and visible minorities among the images indicates the social assumptions of the early carvers. The stone carving includes many symbols of Canada's past as a British and French colony, as well as some purely fanciful characters: above the CARILLON twelve grinning dwarfs play and dance around the Peace Tower. The Centre Block is the only government building in North America where such an extensive program of stone carving has been carried out for so many years. Nearly all the blank stones are now filled, but one remains in the Senate foyer for Queen Elizabeth II.

Strangers

Because of the special privileges accorded to members of Parliament within the House of Commons, everyone who is not an MP is considered a "stranger." Strangers are not permitted on the floor of the Commons chamber or in the members' galleries except by invitation, and the Public Galleries are separated from the chamber by stone pillars and latticework. Historically, strangers were not permitted in the Commons chamber at all, and an MP can still ask that a particular visitor be removed or the galleries be cleared. This happens rarely, but in May 1970 the galleries were cleared when several women chained themselves to the chairs and shouted at the MPs. Strangers sometimes attempt to force their way into the chamber, and in 1964 a spectator threw a container of animal blood onto the floor near the table. Visitors who want to make a political statement will shout or scream at the MPs from the galleries, and in 1962 a spectator burst into "O Canada" in the midst of a debate. In 1879 Mr. J. A. Macdonell, seated on the floor of the House as an honoured guest, called out to a member who was speaking, "You are a cheat and a swindler!" According to the *Annotated Standing Orders*, "the Speaker promptly ordered the floor cleared of all strangers, and the gentleman was expelled, although he re-entered the House by another door soon after. Again ejected, he returned by yet another entrance and was once more ejected by the Sergeant-at-Arms. When he tried to force his way in a third time, the Sergeant-at-Arms barred the way, whereupon Mr. Macdonell sent in a note reiterating his offensive words to the member concerned. For all of this he was eventually taken into custody by the Sergeant-at-Arms and called to the Bar of the House. After he had apologized, he was 'discharged from further attendance.'" *See also*: GALLERIES, PRIVILEGE, SECRECY, SECURITY.

Stornoway

A large, old mansion located at 541 Acacia Avenue in Rockcliffe Park, Stornoway was purchased in 1950 as the official residence of the leader of the Opposition. It is staffed and maintained at public expense, and because of its age and the varying tastes of its frequently changing political tenants it is a popular source of SCANDAL when the redecorating bills get too high. *See also*: 24 SUSSEX DRIVE.

Stornoway, the official Ottawa residence of the leader of the Opposition.

NCC / CCN

24 Sussex Drive

Once the home of a millionaire lumber merchant, 24 Sussex Drive has been the official residence of Canada's prime minister since 1950. Perched on a bluff overlooking the Ottawa River just south of RIDEAU HALL, 24 Sussex is an imposing grey stone house surrounded by a high hedge. It is guarded by the Royal Canadian Mounted Police and is closed to everyone except the prime minister's family, staff, and personal guests. Like Stornoway, 24 Sussex is staffed and maintained at public expense, although the political parties contribute to the personal comforts of particular prime ministers: in 1974 the Liberal Party had a swimming pool installed for Prime Minister Pierre Trudeau, and in the 1980s the Conservative Party paid $300,000 for renovations by Prime Minister Brian Mulroney. Redecorating 24 Sussex is the favourite occupation of prime ministers' wives, and the results are usually expensive and unpopular, especially with the previous and future tenants. Canadians like their prime ministers to be glamorous but frugal, and 24 Sussex is usually a bigger source of SCANDAL than STORNOWAY.

Table

The table on the floor of the House of Commons chamber is the business centre of the Parliamentary process. The Clerk sits at the head of the table, his back to the Speaker. The deputy clerk sits on his right, two table clerks on his left. A chair at the table is provided for the Honorary Officer of the House, usually a retired Clerk. In 1984 this chair was occupied for the first time by former MP Stanley Knowles, who had served in the House for more than forty years as a New Democratic Party MP for Winnipeg North. When the House of Commons is in session, the mace rests on brackets at the lower end of the table. If the mace is not in place, no business can be conducted; when the House sits as a Committee, the mace rests on brackets beneath the table. On the table are reference books and three symbols of the Clerk's office: an inkstand, the House of Commons seal, and a four-sided calendar that enables MPs everywhere in the chamber to see what day it is. All three objects are made of wrought iron, hand-crafted by Montreal artisan Paul Beau (*see:* WROUGHT IRON). Historically, bills and reports submitted to the House were placed on the table for all to read; now documents are mass-produced and circulated to MPs. *See also:* CLERK, MACE.

Taxpayers

The entire cost of the House of Commons and the Senate is paid by the tax-payers of Canada. *See also:* BUDGET

Television

The proceedings of the House of Commons have been televised since 1977; the Senate is not televised. Seven cameras are located in the Commons chamber, three on each side suspended beneath the members' galleries and one facing the Speaker. All cameras are operated remotely from a control room hidden above the public gallery at the south end of the chamber; two sound techicians seated below the gallery control the MPs' microphones – when an MP is speaking, all other microphones are turned off. The debates are broadcast live from coast to coast on the cable TV Parliamentary channel and on Parliament Hill's closed circuit network, OASIS; many outside networks also pick up the signal and use clips for their news broadcasts. The debates are simultaneously recorded on videotape: MPs are later able to watch themselves in action and to get a copy of the video if they wish. Videotapes are made for the public for the cost of the tape, but it is essential to know the date and time of the item requested. The

The television control room high above the Commons chamber. The levers in front operate the seven cameras that cover the Speaker and the 295 MPs below.

MONE CHENG PHOTOGRAPHY STUDIO

videotapes provide a useful way of checking exactly what was said during a debate: an MP can no longer deny an embarrassing mistake and attempt to edit it out of HANSARD.

Portions of the televised debate, particularly QUESTION PERIOD, are seen by millions of Canadians and an MP's career can be profoundly influenced by his physical appearance, language, and behaviour. Yet much of the drama of a debate is not seen on television. The camera focusses only on the member speaking; it is not permitted to cut away to show other MPs shouting, heckling, or making faces, nor is it permitted to zoom in and out on the speaker in case it subliminally "editorializes" on his remarks. All members are deemed equal, regardless of their influence, experience, and ability, and they insist on equality of opportunity on television, however BACKBENCHERS get fewer chances to speak and therefore are less visible on the screen. During Question Period, the prime minister, when present, is always the star.

Television has replaced the READING ROOM as the MPs' primary source of information. An antenna "farm" on the roof of the Wellington building transmits satellite signals from across Canada and the United States through the OASIS cable system: on his office television set an MP can tune into more than a hundred channels and can call up videotapes of recorded programs. The Parliamentary producers record more than fifty news and public-affairs programs every week and create a daily video journal of items they think of political interest. They will not make "home videos" for the MPs or record their fireside chats for their constituents; that is done by a private cable company.

Tourists

Approximately one million people from all over the world visit Parliament Hill every year. A wide range of tourist information is available at the Visitor Information Centre across from Parliament Hill at the corner of Wellington and Metcalfe streets. *See also*: CHANGING OF THE GUARD, INFORMATION, SOUND-AND-LIGHT SHOW.

Tours

Guided tours of the Centre Block are offered every day between 9:00 a.m. and 5:00 p.m. except Christmas, New Year's Day, and Canada Day, July 1. During the summer months – May 24 to September 4, approximately – the tours are extended into the evening hours: no later than 8:00 p.m. weekdays and 9:00 a.m. to 6:00 p.m on weekends. Because of the crowds in the summer, same-day tours should be booked ahead at the Infotent on Parliament Hill. Groups of ten or more can book days or weeks ahead (*see*: GUIDES, INFORMATION). Tours start at the main entrance (*see*: PEACE TOWER) and last thirty to forty-five minutes. They include CONFEDERATION HALL, the FOYERS, antechambers, the CHAMBERS of the House of Commons and the Senate, the HALL OF HONOUR, and the LIBRARY OF PARLIAMENT. If the House of Commons and Senate are in session, access to the foyers and antechambers will be restricted, but visitors are welcome to watch from the public GALLERIES. Tours are given separately in English and French and include a brief explanation of the Canadian political system, as well as details of the architecture and historical background. After the tour, visitors are free to take the elevator to the MEMORIAL CHAMBER in the PEACE TOWER and to the observation deck.

During winter months, tours of the four historical offices in the EAST BLOCK are held on request *on weekends only* between 9:00 a.m. and 4:00 p.m., but in July and August weekday tours can be booked as well at the Infotent between 9:00 a.m. and 8:00 p.m. For anyone interested in Canadian history or the Victorian era, the East Block tour is essential. In the summer, walking tours are

Tourists peek down from the gallery of the Commons foyer. The etched glass ceiling is an elaborate skylight.

RON POLING / CANAPRESS

held on the grounds of Parliament Hill from May to September, leaving on the hour from the Infotent (*see*: STATUES). When tours end, visitors can enter the public galleries if the House of Commons or Senate are in session. The Commons' QUESTION PERIOD is the most fun, and since the crowds are often large and the galleries small, it is preferable to obtain a pass to the members' galleries by contacting an individual MP. The Parliament Buildings are wheelchair accessible and all tours are free.

Ottawa and the surrounding area have several historic sites of political interest: Kingsmere, the former country home of Prime Minister Mackenzie King, is now a museum park and the Speaker's residence; Laurier House, the former home of both Mackenzie King and Prime Minister Sir Wilfrid Laurier, is a museum, and Meech Lake (*see*: CONSTITUTION) is known for its illegal nude bathing beach. *See also*: CHANGING OF THE GUARD, INFORMATION, RIDEAU HALL, SOUND-AND-LIGHT SHOW.

Translation

Since debate in the House of Commons and Senate takes place in both English and French, with one speaker often switching back and forth between languages, simultaneous translation is provided electronically for all MPs, senators, and guests in the galleries. Since the translation is instantaneous and incomplete, it is more accurately called "interpretation." Interpretation for the deaf is provided on the television broadcast. All Parliamentary documents and broadcasts are also produced in both official languages.

Tunnels

In 1960 tunnels were excavated to connect both the West Block and the East Block to the Centre Block. The West Block tunnel has polished stone walls, indirect lighting, air conditioning, and carpet. It enables politicians, aides, and messengers to move around quickly without having to brave rain and blizzards. The dark, unfurnished East Block tunnel is used primiarily by maintenance staff.

U

Unity

Because Canada is a bilingual nation made up of disparate regions, races, religions, and traditions, it is in a constant state of tension caused by competing political forces. Apart from the perpetual search for "the Canadian identity," the struggle for "national unity" is Canada's most obsessive preoccupation. Traditionally, national unity has involved attempting to integrate the minority French-speaking population of Quebec into the rest of the country without destroying its language, culture, or history, and since the 1960s a growing separatist movement in Quebec has campaigned for political independence from Canada. However, Native people are also demanding self-government, and both the western and Atlantic provinces constantly complain about Ottawa. Canada's English-French character has changed dramatically with the arrival of millions of immigrants from around the world, and the historic dialogue between two races is now a multilingual conversation. Canadians take pride in our diversity and in our country, however we define it. *See also*: COLONY, CONFEDERATION, HISTORY.

Unparliamentary

The rules of the House state that "no member shall speak disrespectfully of the Sovereign, nor of any of the Royal Family, nor of the Governor General or the person administering the Government of Canada; nor use offensive words against either House, or against any Member thereof." While insults directed at the Royal Family are extremely rare, members delight in insulting each other, and sessions of both the Commons and the Senate occasionally degenerate into angry shouting matches. Obscene language almost always results in the member being forced to leave the chamber (*see:* NAMING), and an MP who calls another a liar usually apologizes, although some prefer to be expelled rather than retract. Insults can be witty, and MPs are expected to take heckling in their stride, but jokes can misfire: one male cabinet minister who called a woman in the Opposition "baby" was told in no uncertain terms that she was "nobody's baby." Members of Parliament are free to say anything they like in the Commons chamber (*see:* PRIVILEGE) and insults often add to the passion and liveliness of debate. Whether an MP has used "offensive words" must be determined by the Speaker, and being unparliamentary usually means language or behaviour that causes disruption and disorder in the Chamber. It is generally unparliamentary to call another honourable member an ass, a slut, a bastard, son-of-a bitch, fascist, fraud, jerk, racist, hypocrit, idiot, pig, pimp, sambo, scumbag, sleazebag, or turkey, or to accuse him of deceit, fraud, falsehood, murder, manslaughter, verbal diarrhea, or peeing in the wind. *See also:* DECORUM.

V

Vote

A vote in the House of Commons must be held on every bill at second and third reading, and on each amendment proposed during the course of debate; MPs also frequently vote on questions of procedure during debate. Since votes happen so frequently, most are voice votes. The Speaker asks all those in favour or opposed to say "Yea" or "Nay"; the Speaker then decides which side is in the majority. If five or more MPs rise to demand a recorded vote, buzzers ring to summon MPs to the chamber; if the vote is expected, the buzzers sound for fifteen minutes, if not, for thirty minutes. Once the MPs are in their seats the

Speaker puts the question and asks all those in favour to stand. Unless it is a free vote, the members rise by political party, beginning with the leader, and nod to the Speaker as the Clerk calls out their names one by one. Once their votes are recorded, the Speaker calls on those who are opposed to stand and their votes are recorded. The Clerk reports the tally to the Speaker, who declares the motion won or lost. Votes usually split along party lines, but when no one party has a majority in the chamber the result can be unexpected. *See also*: DEFEAT, GOVERNMENT, WHIP.

Voters

Voters must be age eighteen and residents of Canada. Before every general election voters are registered and their names published on a list; each voter also receives a card with the election date, voting hours, and the location of the polling station. Voter turnouts are relatively high, with an average of 75 per cent of eligible voters casting ballots. Women were given the right to vote in 1918, treaty Indians in 1960. Restrictions disqualifying judges and the mentally incompetent were lifted in 1988; the inmates of penitentiaries were enfranchised in 1991. Only election officers in charge of the ballot boxes are not eligible to vote unless there is a tie.

Votes and Proceedings

See: JOURNALS

W

Wednesday

Wednesdays are traditionally a break in the House of Commons routine. Party caucuses meet in the morning and the House sits only from 2:00 p.m. to

8:00 p.m. Night sittings were first abolished on Wednesdays to enable MPs to catch up on their sleep, and for years the Liberal Party had a weekly cocktail party called Wonderful Wednesdays. Caucus meetings followed by a leisurely lunch usually put the MPs and senators in a good humour, and the mood on the Hill tends to be more cheerful on Wednesdays than on other days of the week.

West Block

Built in 1860 as office space for government departments, the West Block lacks the architectural interest and historic associations of the EAST BLOCK. It contains one hidden treasure, the original office of Canada's second prime minister, Alexander Mackenzie (1873-78). Mackenzie was the only prime minister to occupy the West Block – the Mackenzie Tower is named in his honour – and his office, Room 310, is still in use. It is the only office to have survived virtually intact for more than a hundred years, having escaped fire, flood, and renovation. Panelled in carved pine, with a cathedral ceiling and huge bow windows, the office boasts a private washroom in its own little tower and a secret passageway that allows the minister to make a hasty exit.

The West Block under construction in the early 1860s, when Wellington Street was just a mud road. The Ottawa River can be glimpsed behind to the left.

NATIONAL ARCHIVES OF
CANADA / C-10425

Once home to the Department of Public Works, the West Block now houses MPs and cabinet ministers. It contains a popular cafeteria and the Confederation Room, or Room 200, where large public receptions are held. *See also*: BUILDINGS, KITCHEN, RENOVATION, TUNNELS.

Whip

Members of Parliament are independent and strong-minded, and if each MP always voted according to his conscience, no government would be able to sustain a majority in the House. Each party therefore chooses one MP to whip the others into line on party policy and round them up for crucial votes. The whip is the party disciplinarian, and he has almost as much power as the party leader. He keeps a record of each MP's attendance in the House, caucus, and committee and of how the MP votes. He is responsible for knowing where every party member is at all times and what he is doing; if an MP's behaviour threatens to embarrass the party, the whip tries to conceal or correct it. He also warns the leader about possible revolts among BACKBENCHERS and makes their grievances known to the leader. The whip allocates office space to party members and decides who will sit on committees. Whips are not always popular, but a party's success can depend on the whip's ability to charm, cajole, or threaten members into doing what the leader wants.

Women

In 1991, 40 of the 295 MPs were women, 15 of 108 senators. The first woman MP, Agnes Macphail, was elected to the House of Commons in 1921, the first federal election in which women had the vote, although in Manitoba and Alberta

The first woman elected to Canada's Parliament, Agnes Macphail, who sat as an Independent from 1921 until her defeat in 1940.

NATIONAL ARCHIVES OF CANADA / PA 127295

women voted in provincial elections in 1916. The first woman senator, Cairine Wilson, was appointed in 1930 after the Privy Council in Great Britain overturned a ruling by the Supreme Court of Canada that women were not "persons" and therefore could not be appointed to public office. The first woman minister, Ellen Fairclough, was appointed to the cabinet in 1957, and women have subsequently served in senior cabinet positions; both the Senate and the Commons have had women Speakers. In 1989, Audrey McLaughlin of the New Democratic Party became the first woman to lead a major national party; Canada has had one woman provincial premier but not a woman prime minister. A bronze bust of Agnes Macphail is in the Speaker's corridor of the House of Commons, and a bust of Cairine Wilson is in the anteroom to the Senate chamber, which also contains a plaque commemorating the five women from Alberta who fought and won the "Persons' Case."

Wood Carving

The chambers of the House of Commons and the Senate and the Library of Parliament are famous for their beautiful wood carving, yet the names of the individual carvers are unknown. During construction, the contracts for oak or pine wall panels, doors, shelves, desks and chairs were given to several different carpentry firms, and the task of carving was assigned to their workmen. The House of Commons currently has a carver in

A superb example of the fine wood carving to be found in the Library of Parliament, the Commons chamber, and the Senate. The figure appears to be wearing moccasins.

CHRIS LUND/NATIONAL ARCHIVES OF CANADA / PA-185327

The wrought-iron filigree on the roof of the East Block imaginatively captures Canada's taditional floral themes: the rose, shamrock, thistle, and the fleur-de-lis.

CHRIS LUND / NATIONAL ARCHIVES
OF CANADA / PA-185325

its carpentry shop; he undertakes special assignments such as carving the beaver on the altar in the MEDITATION ROOM.

Wrought Iron

The Parliament buildings contain many examples of wrought-iron work handcrafted by Paul Beau of Montreal between 1919 and 1926. Influenced by Art Nouveau and the designs of William Morris in England, Beau made elaborate fenders and fire irons for the ministers' fireplaces, but many examples of his work were lost when the fireplaces were sealed or boarded up. His most prized pieces are the House of Commons' seal, inkstand, and calendar on the table in the Commons chamber. The square ink-bottle rests in the clutches of four large griffons, and the seal is engraved with the head of a beaver drawn from a Haida design. Wrought-iron grills and gates form an important part of the Gothic decoration in the Parliament buildings; one of the finest examples is the upper part of the wall along Wellington Street, constructed in 1873.

X

In an election, ballots must be marked with an X opposite the name of only one candidate. Ballots marked in any other way will be spoiled.

Yea

When the Speaker calls a voice vote, those in favour call out "Yea," those opposed, "Nay." *See*: VOTE.

Zzzzzzzz

A sound sometimes heard in the chamber of the Commons or the Senate. It is always associated with the OTHER PLACE. *See also*: SPEECH.